1

The car crawled from one set of traffic lights to the next along the busy main road. Dark clouds tumbled down the hills to cast a bleak shadow over the town. Ella thought her mum was quiet and looked a bit tense. She had listened to Ella's school gossip without comment. She was unconcerned about Mr Merrilee dropping his coffee cup in the classroom, or that Jenny Rees had come to school with green tinged hair and had been immediately sent home. It wasn't until the car turned into her grandfather's street that Ella realised that something unusual was going on. Her dad's car was parked on the drive next to grandfather's.

"Why have we come to Grandad's?" she asked, then added, "Why is Dad here?"

A sense of foreboding descended on Ella as her mother parked the car half on, half off the pavement across the entrance to the drive and turned off the engine.

Her mother sighed.

"Wait until we get in, Ella," she said in a strained voice as she collected bits and pieces that had tumbled out of her handbag. She checked her face and hair in the rear view mirror and sighed again.

Katrina was forty-two years old with deep blue eyes that

were a shade darker than her father's. The crow's feet around her eyes were testament to a lifestyle steeped in laughter. Her skin, fair and remarkably toned for her age, contrasted with a natural blue-grey hair that was closely cropped and spiked. A slash of scarlet red lipstick, the shade that caused most men to turn and look again and some women to wonder how she managed to get away with it, brightened her face, giving the impression that she knew what she wanted and usually got it. However, it was a facade. She knew what she wanted alright, but she suffered from indecision. She sighed again, then spent a second collecting her thoughts before getting out.

Ella threw open the car door and without waiting for her mother walked to the ornate, wooden entrance to the large detached house that stood at the head of a small, mature cul-de-sac. Her grandfather opened the door.

Harry Crimson wore brown checked slippers, brown chinos and a beige checked shirt that hung outside his trousers. His grey hair and blue rimmed spectacles surrounded deep blue eyes and a round face that bore a full days growth of beard. His weak smile reflected the sombre mood of his granddaughter. He hugged her in a warm but limp embrace before uttering his usual greeting.

"Hello, Tuppence," he said. It was a nickname he had given her as a very small child.

Ella loved her grandad. He was caring and playful, kind and generous, and she was the apple of his eye. She put her arms around him and hugged him back. There was a fear within her that threatened towards hysteria. Something was wrong, very wrong, and she couldn't figure out what it could be. For one thing, her grandad appeared to be awkward with her. That wasn't like him at all. He was usually funny, gently chiding her about a possible boyfriend or something.

Panic rose within her. Something was definitely wrong,

but what? What was the most awful thing that could have happened? A thought struck her. Perhaps someone had died. Dread overwhelmed her. Mentally, she collated a list of those relatives and friends of the family who were in ill health. In an instant she began ticking people off the list. Then another thought invaded her thinking. Had the death been sudden? If that was the case, then it could be anyone. In those few short moments a catalogue of people burst through her mind. Pictures flooded her consciousness. Obviously it wasn't her mum or dad, or her grandad. So no-one really close then, she thought. Ella's grandma had died several years ago, when Ella was a lot younger, and she was an only child so she wasn't very close to her cousins. The dead person had to be one of her dad's brothers or sisters, or one of their children, her cousins. Maybe it was her gran, her dad's mum. She was a nasty piece of work, or so her mother had said on more than one occasion. Grandpa had died two years earlier but Ella had never had a loving relationship with him. They'd lived too far away for them to be regular visitors, in any case Grandpa had been unwelcome in her house because he was a pipe smoker who refused to compromise his habits on the grounds that he was old and he could do what he liked.

Having weighed through the possibilities and made several assumptions based on age and ill health, she came to the conclusion that it must be her gran that had died and they were trying to break the news to her gently. Inwardly, she was relieved that she'd sorted it out. She'd show a bit of shock, a bit of remorse, cry a little, hug her dad a lot, then they could all go for a pizza on the way back home.

She walked into the hall and stood next to the full length mirror near the hat stand, an ornate relic that had stood there for years. She kicked off her shoes – a rule that Grandad had brought in several years ago when he'd bought a brand new, beige, wool carpet. Most people ignored it now but she still honoured the ruling simply because her grandad did. She briefly caught sight of her own reflection.

She was small and slim with deep brown hair that shimmered in the light. Her blue uniform didn't do her justice. Ella had the shape of a vibrant young woman, but the uniform was androgynous. She wore no make-up – not because it was a school rule but because she didn't need it. Her eyes were large and the same deep blue as her grandad's. Her nose was aquiline, like her father's, and she had the flawless skin and even temperament of her mother.

She walked down the hall in stockinged feet.

Just before she entered the lounge another thought struck her. What if she was wrong and it wasn't her gran that had died? And then another question formed. Why were they breaking the news to her at Grandad's? She didn't have time to reconsider the options. She clutched her school bag tightly in both hands and entered the lounge. She was breathing so deeply that she was on the verge of hyperventilating.

The room was warm. A real fire roared in the fireplace, the flames reflected in the face of a clock on the opposite wall. The corners of the room looked dark and foreboding. Shadows accentuated the grim expression set on Ella's father's face. He smiled a mirthless smile at his daughter and gestured her to sit down.

Oliver, Ella's dad, had never been demonstrative in his love for Ella, although he loved her deeply. The fault lay in his upbringing according to his wife. His mother had been a believer in the adages 'children should be seen and not heard' and 'spare the rod and spoil the child', but not only that, she considered that children should be obedient and respectful and should never speak until spoken to.

"What's going on?" Ella enquired tentatively.

The eyes of the adults in the room shot glances at each other, each deciding who should speak first. The silence lasted for a few seconds while Ella searched for clues on their faces.

It was Harry who spoke first, addressing his daughter. "Katrina, are you going to explain to Ella why we're all here?" His voice was soft and soothing, to take away any sting that might be forthcoming. He was trying to set the tone.

Ella fixed her eyes on her mother.

"I … we …" she mumbled, searching for the right words.

She sat down heavily in an armchair, defeated by the moment.

"Oh, for Heaven's sake!" shouted Oliver suddenly, his anger rushing to the surface, instantly breaking the false ambiance generated by Harry. He turned to Ella and said, "Your mother …"

Oliver!" interjected Harry. "Let me remind you what we agreed. These are sensitive issues. Think of Ella." His stony stare and clipped tone were sufficient to admonish him. Harry wasn't going to let this get out of hand. Whatever happened today, he wasn't going to allow Ella to suffer any more than she had to.

Oliver turned away and shook his head.

Ella started to cry. "What's happened?" she pleaded. Anxiety stole across her face, fear taking up residence in her eyes. "I'm getting frightened. Mum? Dad?"

Harry reached out and firmly embraced her. He knelt down and put his hand under her chin. He looked at Katrina and Oliver and shook his head in exasperation. They were both capable of doing lots of wonderfully complicated things yet they couldn't tell their daughter a simple truth. With sad, tired eyes he looked at his granddaughter and said softly. "Your mum and dad are having some difficulties."

He coughed to rid himself of a lump that had gathered in his throat. "They've decided that these difficulties need a bit of time to sort out, and that it would probably be better if they spent some time apart."

Katrina began to sob. Oliver exhaled loudly, folded his arms, stared into the fire and muttered, "Huh".

Ella's body lost energy. She sank against her grandfather, clinging on as though he was about to disappear. Surprisingly, she felt relief that nobody had died, but after a few brief seconds the momentary relief turned to anxiety again, then fear. What was Grandad talking about? Difficulties? What difficulties? Spending time apart? Where will I go? What's going to happen to me?

"C'mon, Tuppence," Harry said, "let's get some milk and a chocolate digestive." He released his hold and guided Ella towards the kitchen, leaving the uncommunicative adults wrestling with their social inadequacies.

Ella followed helplessly.

Ordinarily she wouldn't have been allowed to have such things as a chocolate digestive between meals. Actually, she didn't want a biscuit, or milk for that matter, but she sensed that her grandad was somehow being diplomatic and allowed herself to be shepherded into the kitchen.

Harry closed the door behind him and asked her if she wanted warm or cold milk, then answered his own question. "Warm I reckon."

Ella looked out of the window. In the distance she could see people walking through the park as if nothing had happened. Their lives hadn't changed like hers. They were probably loved and had nice homes to go to. They would be saving for a family holiday or a weekend away. Just like normal families. She didn't belong to a normal family anymore. Something had happened to change that. 'Difficulties' had occurred, whatever that meant.

The microwave pinged and Harry removed the glass of milk and placed it on the table next to a plate with four chocolate biscuits on it. Ella smiled a tiny smile. Her grandad never let anyone eat a chocolate biscuit by themselves.

Ella dipped her biscuit in the warm milk and glanced at her grandad. She wasn't allowed to dunk.

Harry half-smiled back. There was mistiness in his eyes. His hand covered hers as he whispered, "Things will work themselves out, Tuppence. They have a habit of doing that."

Suddenly the front door slammed. Ella jumped at the sound.

"You stay here," Harry said. "I'll see what's going on."

He left Ella sitting at the table. She didn't want him to leave. She felt all alone, abandoned even. She heard the muffled voices of her mother and her grandad and then a brief period of silence before the kitchen door opened and they both entered the room. Her mother was red-eyed. She sat awkwardly next to Ella and put her elbows on the table and cradled her head in her hands. Her engagement ring sparkled on her finger. Her wedding band was worn and dull beside it. She wiped her eyes.

"There's a lot of explaining to do," Katrina said, "and to be honest I don't know how to do it." Her voice was strained and full of subdued emotion. "I've never been in a situation like this before." She shrugged helplessly. "I'm not happy and I haven't been happy for some time."

She paused to wipe away another tear and glanced at her father. She saw in his expression that she wasn't making sense. She turned to Ella, who looked completely perplexed. She gulped in a lungful of air and gathered herself.

"I can't go into details at the moment," she said more forcefully. "It may have been wrong not to tell you what was going on, but please believe me, I was only trying to protect you."

Ella's brow furrowed.

Katrina looked away to seek some sort of inspiration, and found it lurking in the back of her mind.

"Ella, you know how Dad and I have been arguing a lot lately ..."

Ella nodded. It was true. Little things had started annoying them. Her dad had spent long periods in the study, on the computer, then even more time at work. Weekends had been family occasions in the past, but now they seemed to be secondary considerations. She couldn't remember the last time they'd been out for a drive in the country or had a day by the seaside. When was the last time they'd been to London, or any other city, for a sight-seeing trip? It had been a long time ago.

She knew he was a high powered executive, but why couldn't he do all that stuff at work and not bring it home? He went to work early enough and stayed later than most. Her mum had mentioned a few times that they'd had to decline invitations to parties and social events because her dad couldn't, or wouldn't, go and she felt embarrassed going to formal occasions without him simply because she'd have to explain that he was at work. By definition that meant he considered his work to be more important than the wedding, birthday or party.

The flip side of that was that her father's absence had allowed her to spend time with her mum, and she had loved that.

"Is this about him being at work or in the study all the time?" she asked.

"Well, partly," Katrina stammered, "but there are other things as well."

"Like what?" Ella asked, getting straight to the point.

Katrina didn't want to get involved in a discussion at this stage; there were some things she had yet to accept about her own culpability in the matter.

"Ella, this isn't the time to go into details. Suffice to say that both your dad and I have had a few long discussions about how we feel about each other, and neither of us is satisfied with our lives together. The only thing we can agree about at the moment is you. We both love you very dearly and of course we want the best for you."

Ella didn't think she was very convincing; it was just the right thing to say. "Obviously not," she said, "or else you would still be together. What am I going to tell my friends? What about school?"

Harry shuffled uncomfortably. This wasn't going well. He was having difficulty following Katrina's thoughts. It appeared that Katrina was explaining things without actually saying anything.

Katrina said, "Ella, these are difficult times for all of us. We both know that you're terribly upset and we're trying to minimise the impact of this situation on you. We love you very much. It's just that we're not too sure about loving each other at the moment."

Ella glanced at her grandad. He shrugged his shoulders and made himself busy tidying up what didn't need to be tidied. He looked older now than he'd appeared at any time during her life. He dragged his feet around the kitchen, each step heavier than the previous one.

As he restacked plates and rearranged the coffee mugs, Harry felt every one of his sixty-five years. What's more, he felt redundant, powerless, inept. He'd never been very good in these situations. He usually let people get on with their own affairs. But this was his family. It was his daughter, her husband and his beloved Ella. She shouldn't have to go through this. He felt as if he wasn't doing his job as a father and grandfather properly and resented the fact that he didn't know what was going on. If he knew, then he could do a better job of protecting Ella from this rubbish.

Katrina saw the same man that her daughter saw – but in a different way. She saw the loving parent who had instilled in her the values that she was trying to teach her daughter, although he had done a far better job than she. He was a man that hated confrontation of any sort, but he possessed a steely determination that had surprised many people. When the chips were down, it was people like her father that made the difference. But at that particular moment he was a shattered replica of the man who had raised her. She felt a pang of guilt.

She idly shredded her damp tissue until it became a mess in the palm of her left hand. She scrunched it up and wandered over to the kitchen bin and deposited it through the swing top before selecting a piece of kitchen roll as a replacement. She resumed her seat next to Ella.

"Darling," she said softly as she touched Ella's hair, "sometimes we do things because we have to, sometimes because we want to, and other times because we need to. I don't have to leave your father because I have to, or want to; I need to do this for me – just for me."

She looked deeply into Ella's eyes, silently imploring her to understand.

"All of your life I've put your needs first. After that, I did what your father wanted to do. By the time it came round to me, there wasn't a lot left."

Her eyes stole a glance at her father, who was leaning against the sink staring blankly out of the window.

"It's only recently that I've started to think about what I wanted out of life. I'm forty-two years old and I've got this feeling that the world is passing me by. I know it's a cliché but I asked myself what will life be like five years from now, and I'm sorry to say I didn't like the answer."

She paused to let the information sink in before continuing.

"You'll be at university. Your father will be at work all the time. What will I do? I gave up a career to bring you up, to look after the house and be the boss's wife. I don't want that anymore. I want to be me for a change. I want to be known as Katrina, not Ella's mum or Oliver's wife, or, for that matter, Harry Crimson's daughter, no matter how good those names are. Your dad doesn't see how that changes things. You might say the same. But it means a lot to me."

Ella looked at her frightened, lonely mother. The depth of her emotion was obvious but Ella still didn't appreciate the reasons for it. Mum was Mum. Of course she was Katrina, what difference did that make? Dad made lots of money and Mum could do what she liked. Her mother was a lovely mum. Her friends had said on many occasions that they wished their mums were like hers. For her mother to be in such a state as this meant that something was dreadfully wrong. Whatever it was, she knew that her mother wouldn't have caused this situation without justification.

She reached across to her mother and hugged her like the frightened girl she was and the frightened little girl she used to be. They sobbed in each other's arms.

The damp-eyed old man in the room silently laid a loving hand on each of their shoulders.

2

It had been agreed that Ella would stay at Harry's house for the time being. The adults had agreed that she needed stability, and that she couldn't be guaranteed that at home. Neither of her parents wanted her to be anxious about what was going on in the house, especially as her mother had moved into the spare room.

It had been difficult for Ella to try and have a normal evening in an abnormal setting. She was familiar with the house, course; it was almost a second home, but it wasn't *her* home. It didn't have *her* bed and duck-down duvet. It didn't have the mirrored wardrobes and funky décor. It didn't have her posters and diary, her clothes, books and cuddly toys. She was a million miles and several light years away from reality. The world that had existed five hours before still survived beyond the front door of her grandad's house, but it didn't seem like *her* world anymore.

Sitting up in bed, she held her favourite book: a very old copy of *Grimm's Fairy Tales*, which she'd kept at her grandad's place since she was a little girl.

It had originally been given to her grandad on his eleventh birthday. He'd often told her that it was a present he'd cherished since that day. He'd become a member of the local library on his tenth birthday. There, he'd discovered the intoxicating world of books and spent many hours poring over lavish pictures in encyclopaedias that contained interesting facts and articles. When the internet arrived, he had sagely shook his head and declared the death of all libraries. On some occasions he'd gone one step further and stated that beautiful books would shortly become a thing of the past. The reality was different.

Ella was a rather infrequent guest at the house nowadays. But in years gone by, her grandad had been her favourite babysitter when her parents were away on business, or during mid-term holidays. From the time she was brought to the house to the time she left, her grandad looked after her, cherished her and celebrated her. They made up and sang little songs. They told each other stories and pretended they were everyone from pirates to pixies. He had given her his volume of *Grimm's Fairy Tales* on her eleventh birthday. It contained dozens of her favourite tales and it remained in her grandad's house for whenever she visited. But as she grew older, the stay-overs tailed off and the window on the imaginary world it contained receded.

There was a knock on the door.

"Come in, Grandad."

The door opened and Harry peered in. "Hello, Tuppence," he said. "Just wanted to know if you would like a warm drink or something before you dropped off."

Ella shook her head. "No thanks."

Harry waited a moment. "Everything ok?" he asked tentatively.

"Well, my life's falling apart, but other than that everything is just dandy."

Harry forced a smile and said, "Mind if I sit down?" He nodded towards the foot of the bed.

"Of course," Ella said. "Just like the old times."

Old times indeed, Harry thought. He'd spent many an hour sitting on the foot of this bed watching her sleep, as a child, when she'd been suffering from measles or whooping cough or some other medical disaster. It wasn't because Oliver and Katrina couldn't manage or anything, it was just that his late wife, Thelma, insisted on looking after Ella whenever she was poorly.

"Just like the old times," he muttered as he sat down. "I wish that were true." He made himself comfortable and looked around the room. "I haven't touched this room for years," he said, noticing flaking paint on the walls. "Could do with a once over. I remember when I last painted it. You must've been about nine or ten." He pointed to the back of the room. "We bought that bookcase to keep all your books in, and that wardrobe for your clothes. Your grandma was keen to have all new things ready for your first stay."

Ella followed her grandad's eyes as they did a tour of the room, no doubt watching his former self assembling and painting. It didn't take much to get her grandad reminiscing. Sometimes he sat in his chair and carefully revisited chosen memories for what seemed like ages.

A long moment passed before Ella broke the silence. "Grandad, do you think Mum and Dad will get back together?"

It was a big question, and something Harry couldn't predict. He didn't want to fob Ella off with a speech about the uncertainties of life and the madness of prediction. He shrugged. It wasn't an easy call to make so he decided to tell it as he saw it.

"I don't know, Tuppence," he said. "I don't know what your mum and dad have talked about."

"What? You have no idea at all? I find that hard to believe. Mum always talks to you."

Ella was right. Harry had instilled in his daughter the belief that whatever happened in life, good or bad, your parents would always love you and try their best to help you out. He considered the bond between parent and child as eternal. However, on this occasion he had the distinct feeling that he wasn't in receipt of all the facts.

He coughed to clear his throat.

"There are some things that happen between couples that can't usually be discussed with their parents," he said, "as you'll no doubt find out when you grow up. Couples have private things to talk about, if you see what I mean."

"Like sex and stuff," Ella said candidly.

Harry studied her face. She was fifteen years old. She had the body of a young woman, with a keen, albeit egocentric, mind. Emotionally, she was still a little naive. She would know a bit about sex and probably have some romantic notions about love and relationships.

"Yes," he admitted, "stuff like that is one example, but not what I was thinking about." He paused to gather his thoughts. "If we meet a special person, then we share our hopes, dreams and ambitions with them. We build a life, and sometimes we fail doing that. A lot of people give up at that stage, but most just plough on and learn from the experience. Sometimes we have to rebuild that relationship, or build new dreams, because life has a tendency to kick you in the teeth when you least expect it."

It was a statement filled with truth, although he didn't know if Ella had the maturity to consider the ramifications of what he'd said.

He stood up and adjusted the lamp shade, which was a little out of kilter, before resuming.

"Sometimes you do things that you know are wrong, or you know will fail. But you still do it. What I'm trying to say here is that we all make mistakes. That might be through bad judgement or wrong decisions. Sometimes, we just have a bad day and everything seems to go wrong."

Ella looked puzzled. She was trying to understand what her grandfather was saying but was only grasping vague inferences.

Harry resumed his seat on the bed.

"I don't know if any of that applies to your mum and dad, but you have to consider the possibility that something has gone disastrously wrong somewhere – and it may never be fixed."

He was being realistic. He was saying things off the top of his head that were purely speculative but anchored in past experience.

Ella planted her chin firmly on her chest but didn't cry.

"People don't like to admit they've done anything they're ashamed of," Harry continued. "The person they won't tell is their nearest and dearest. If your mother is at fault for something, she won't tell me until it's all in the open. I have my suspicions," he said sagely, "but I won't discuss them until I'm asked.

"Suspicions about what?"

Harry regretted having said that. It was true he'd thought about what had brought this situation about and he'd come to the conclusion, rightly or wrongly, that infidelity was the key issue at the heart of the matter. And he suspected Katrina wasn't telling him the truth.

"Nothing at the moment," he said, raising the flat of his hand towards Ella as if signalling a car to stop like a traffic policeman. "But I'll promise you this. There's an awful lot more to come out of this, mark my words. When the cards are on the table, we'll talk some more and get things straightened out. I won't lie to you, Ella. I won't pull any punches. You're right. From this moment on, the world is a different place, for all concerned."

"But Grandad …"

"No, Ella," Harry interrupted, "I won't talk anymore about the subject until more is known."

He relieved her of the *Grimm's Fairy Tales* book and forced a smile. "Aah, now this is definitely a flash from the past." He riffled the pages from back to front and stopped randomly at 'The Peasant's Wise Daughter'. "Oh yes, I remember this story. She was a crafty girl that one. She put the king in his place didn't she?"

Ella looked over his shoulder at the gothic picture depicting the story. "It's not my favourite, Grandad."

Harry continued fanning the pages, letting out the occasional aah or chuckle.

Ella was overcome with sadness. She had an odd feeling of *déjà vu* and was whisked back five years to a time when she was ill in bed and her grandad had told her a fairy tale to comfort her when she was feeling sorry for herself.

"Tell me a story, Grandad, like you used to when I was a little girl."

Ella's voice had become tiny, whether real or imagined, Harry couldn't tell.

"Which one do you want?" he asked, holding the book in the air for her to decide.

"Why don't you tell me one I haven't heard before," she said. "Your stories are much better anyway."

He chuckled at the soft-soaped compliment. She had always been very good at manipulating situations.

"Well, you've put me on the spot now, Tuppence. It's been ages since I invented a story for you. You're much older now. I can't kid you anymore."

"Oh c'mon, Grandad."

"Alright, alright. You snuggle down into your duvet and I'll think of something. Sure you don't want a drink?

Ella shook her head and settled down.

Harry rubbed his chin. For a brief moment Ella was ten years old again, Thelma was downstairs making some tea with a boiled egg and 'soldiers' for supper, and he was babysitting his poorly granddaughter.

"Right. Ok. I think I have something." He cleared his throat theatrically. "Are you lying comfortably?" he asked in a mock serious tone.

Ella nodded.

Then, in his best storytelling voice, Harry said, "Then we'll begin. Once upon a time …"

"Grandad!" Ella reprimanded. "Just because I ask for a fairy tale doesn't mean it has to begin that way."

Harry chuckled. "Ok, Tuppence. Here we go then."

***

There was a young girl called Lela who lived in a place not far away. Her father was a nobleman who rode all over the kingdom helping people to make sure they lived safely and in peace. People used to travel many miles to see him and hear his words. Afterwards, they would talk to each other and comment on how wise he was. He was called Rivelo.

His wife was called Inkarta, and she was Lela's mother. She was also well loved and she often visited the people in their villages and helped them in any way she could. She always took her magic mouse wherever she went. People used to stop her in the street and ask to see the mouse. She would dig deep into her sack and bring him out to show them. However, whenever the magic mouse was brought into the sunlight it used to disappear. Some people said she was lying and that there was no such creature as the magic mouse, but Inkarta wasn't lying; only she knew the truth. Inkarta loved Rivelo, but her daughter was the apple of her eye and she loved her dearly.

For many years they lived a happy existence together in a castle just south of a great river. Every day, the sun rose and shone its light and warmth on the castle and that had the effect of making everyone in it and everyone who entered it a happy person. But the magic mouse was never seen. When it was the dead of night, the magic mouse would come out of the sack and play. It would run and dance and squeak. It often used to wake Lela up, but she never saw it.

One day Lela got up and looked out of the window and was astonished to see a dark cloud on the horizon. She saw that it was coming towards the castle. She quickly got ready and ran through the kitchen, past her mother and father who were having breakfast.

"There's a dark cloud," she shouted. "I'm going to see where it's going."

"Be careful," said her father, who was having a slice of toast before he set off for the day.

"Watch what you're doing," said her mother anxiously. She had seen dark clouds before, but they had always gone away. It meant that something bad was going to happen if it stopped above you. The cloud had passed over the castle and settled on the village.

She turned to her husband and said, "Where are you going today?"

This was the question she asked every day.

"Over the hills and far away," he said.

This was what he replied every day.
"When will you be back?" she asked.
Always her second question.
"When the day ends and night begins," he said.
Always his second answer.

Lela ran to the local village, keeping an eye on the dark cloud, which seemed to hover above it. She was disappointed to find that nothing had changed there. It wasn't even raining. She searched high and low but found nothing at all except a man looking for somewhere to stay for a while.

Someone told him to go to the edge of the village, where he would find somewhere to live and some work. As he walked away Lela watched him. He was a quiet, distinguished-looking man who carried a black sack in either hand, with a large book tucked under his right arm.

Lela looked up into the sky and saw that the dark cloud had moved again and was getting smaller. She decided that the cloud wasn't as interesting as she had first thought, so she ran back to the castle to tell her mother.

Inkarta welcomed her home and listened intently to her daughter's news. That would be the most exciting part of her day.

Rivelo came home late. He had been to a village far away and spoken great words to everyone there. He was lauded and praised for his wisdom. He was pleased with himself. He was a big man. His name was well known. He was doing what he planned to do all his life. Soon, he would be the biggest of all men. He was happy.

But recently Inkarta had complained to him that

he spent too long riding about the country and not spending enough time with her in the castle. He'd told her to go into the country and help people as he did. People would let her help because she was his wife and Lela's mother. He was happy to let her go, but he wanted her to be home for him returning from his travels.

One evening Inkarta greeted him with a kiss. "How has today been?" she asked.

Always her first question.

"Good," he replied "The people are happier now that I have spoken to them."

Always his first reply.

They ate their meal together. Lela talked of the dark cloud. Rivelo spoke of all the people who praised him. Inkarta remained silent.

When Lela went to bed, Rivelo said, "Why are you quiet?"

Inkarta said, "I have nothing to say."

"Why?" he asked without thinking.

"I do not go out into the wide world and meet anyone. I do not see anyone except my family. I have no-one to talk to except my mouse," she replied with a sigh.

Rivelo wished he hadn't brought the subject up. "Go and find something that will interest you. I have no objections. Just make sure that Lela and I are not disadvantaged by it."

That evening, when Lela and Rivelo were sleeping, Inkarta got up and took her sack into another room. The room had letters and numbers engraved on the floor tiles.

She took the magic mouse out of the sack and although she couldn't see it, she could hear it scurrying around the floor. Soon it crept over to the tiles and started to scamper quickly between them. Inkarta heard its feet scratching furiously on the tiles until each letter glowed in ghostly green.

Each tile's luminescence waxed and waned in turn to spell out words. Inkarta wrote the words down and hid the message away.

She put the magic mouse back into the sack and went back to bed.

The next day, Inkarta went into the village to look around. There was another dark cloud in the sky, although it was smaller than the previous one. She wasn't bothered by it as it didn't hover over her.

The first thing she came across was a stall in the village market. The stall was new, and so was the man running it. He looked quiet and distinguished. He was selling clothing and other things. She spoke to him and he revealed that his name was Estraneo and he collected things that people usually threw away.

"Someone's rubbish used to be someone's treasure," he said, "and those things can be treasured by someone else."

He spoke sense. Inkarta immediately liked him. She told him she was looking for opportunities to meet with people. He smiled and asked her to visit the stall whenever she liked because she would meet lots of people and she could help them. She accepted.

When she told Lela and Rivelo, they were both pleased for her.

The days turned into weeks and the conversation around the table at meal times became dominated by Inkarta's experiences, and her visits to the tiled room with the magic mouse became more frequent.

The stall became bigger and Inkarta spent more time there. Estraneo set up more stalls across the market and was soon revered by the villagers.

Occasionally he had to leave the village and go to other villages. One day he came to Inkarta and said, "I'm closing the stalls for two days next week to go to a big city. I want you to come with me."

Inkarta had been to cities before, but didn't like them because there were too many people and she couldn't talk to them all. She would've liked to have gone, but she didn't think Rivelo would like it.

When she thought more about it later that day she realised that if she went away with Estraneo, her personal feelings might get out of control. She realised that she looked forward to seeing him every day, and she missed him when he wasn't there. She knew that he felt the same about her. It was exciting and exhilarating, but it was also very wrong. However, when she mentioned to Rivelo about the visit, he agreed that it was a good opportunity to learn more about cities and to meet more people.

Inkarta was undecided. She waited until it was dark and took the sack to the room of tiles.

***

Harry stopped, got up off the bed and straightened the duvet cover.

Ella gave him a puzzled look. "That's a funny story," she said.

"I'm not laughing," Harry said.

"Not that kind of funny," Ella said. "I meant funny peculiar. You didn't even finish it."

"Well, have a think about it and we'll finish it off tomorrow, perhaps."

Ella was tired. It had been a long drawn out day and she didn't argue. "Ok, Grandad. Nite nite."

Nite nite had been her last epithet every night she'd stayed there as a little girl.

"Nite nite, Tuppence," Harry said as he bent over and kissed Ella's forehead.

He switched off the light and shut the door behind him. He went downstairs and secured the house. He poured himself a glass of milk and then headed back upstairs to his bedroom. It had been a long day and he feared there would be many more of them.

The story he'd tried to tell Ella was a poor one. He was out of practise. He hadn't finished it because the story it related to wasn't complete yet either. Would Ella guess that she was part of it?

3

Friday's dawn broke to reveal a glorious May sunrise. A fresh breeze provided a memory of April but promised a taste of summer sun. By the time Ella went down for breakfast the smell of frying bacon teased and tantalised the taste buds. The table was all set, and tea was in the pot. Surprisingly, she refused the bacon sandwich, or the alternatives of boiled eggs and cereal, and settled for two slices of toast with a cup of tea.

Harry ate two thick bacon sandwiches with a dollop of sauce on each.

"So what was that all that about, then?" asked Ella as she nibbled at a slice of toast lightly coated with butter.

"What was all what about?" Harry said between mouthfuls.

"The story last night."

"It's just a story."

"It was quite strange."

Harry raised his eyebrows. "You think my story is strange! You must have forgotten some of the Grimm's stories. Some of those are more than strange. Anyone dipping into a Grimm's fairy tale would be bombarded by images and ideas of murder, slavery and savagery in a multitude of guises. In contrast, my story is timid."

Ella kept on at him. "That's true. But that wasn't one of theirs. It was one of yours."

She had a piercing look in her eyes.

"How does it end?" she asked.

Harry feigned innocence. He wasn't going to spill the beans just yet. He didn't have enough information, or suspicion, to give away leads.

"I have no idea," he said. "I just make it up as I go along."

Ella wasn't satisfied with that, but let it go.

"So when's the next instalment?"

Harry smiled his reassuring grandad smile and said, "Whenever we can fit it in. Tonight or tomorrow maybe?"

"Ok," Ella said. "I'll keep you to it."

The telephone rang and Harry went into the hall to answer it. He reappeared after a few moments and said softly, "It's your dad. He wants to have a word."

Ella grimaced. She didn't fancy having a heart-to-heart chat with her dad at this time of day. Not before she went to school. The last thing she wanted was to be upset. She quickly got up anyway and hurried into the hall.

Harry shut the door behind her to give her some privacy. The fact was, he didn't want to overhear the conversation. He was in a difficult situation. He liked Oliver. He was a decent bloke who had made his daughter happy, or so he had thought. Sure enough they'd had rows and disagreements like everyone else, but on the whole Oliver was a good son-in-law to him and a great dad to Ella.

Ella had been right when she'd said her mother always talked to him if she had a problem. Katrina had mentioned that she was having 'difficulties' and he had counselled her to seek ways of sorting it out. She had complained of Oliver's long periods of doing work related things and had said that although he was earning a lot of money, they were drifting apart. After much discussion and talking through a plethora of alternatives, he had said to her that she needed to find something to do, such as a hobby, a club or worthwhile cause. He knew from past experience that Katrina usually immersed herself in activities, and something along those lines would act as a distraction. Of course it wouldn't fix any problems they had between them as individuals.

Over the next few months Katrina had heeded his advice and sought new experiences. She developed an interest in a local charity that was only too glad to recruit someone with the drive, skill and enthusiasm that Katrina possessed.

Katrina's complaints about Oliver ceased, and Harry though his advice was working. She'd not stopped talking about the charity and how it was raising funds. She had volunteered to staff stalls at fairs and community events, and had even agreed to serve in the High Street shop, where they had only one permanent member of staff. The others were all like her: volunteers.

Katrina had reported that the shop was busy and well organised, and was seen as an exemplar of what could be done. It wasn't until she was invited to a three day regional conference that the seeds of doubt were sown in Harry's mind. She'd been asked to attend as a representative of the volunteer sector, with her High Street shop manager, a man called Will. Soon it was 'Will says this, Will says that, or Will wouldn't do that'. The conference was paid for, with accommodation and meals provided. Katrina loved it. However, Harry had detected a slight change in her attitude when she'd returned home. She was exceptionally affectionate towards Oliver and Ella. She suggested they go away as a family to experience a bit of what she called 'togetherness'.

He'd kept his own counsel. One day he had walked into the shop and browsed through the stuff on offer. The shop wasn't particularly busy, a handful of people with time on their hands and disposable income to spend were milling about, just like him.

A tall, plumpish man in his mid-forties stood near the till. He looked dour and doleful, but that changed when someone asked him a question or wanted assistance. His smile beamed and his eyes lit up. There was an intelligence there that was easily missed. Harry'd wondered if this was Will. Surely not. He'd finished browsing and, with a casual nod at the man, had left without buying anything.

His next conversation with Katrina established that the man had indeed been called William, and his concerns were alleviated. He was so different from Oliver. He wasn't even in the same league.

And then all this had blown up. Katrina and Oliver had had a row and several accusations had been made, including an alleged affair between Katrina and Will. Katrina had vehemently denied it, of course, but his gut feeling wasn't dispelled. Oliver wasn't convinced either, but he had no proof at all. The arguments demonstrated that the relationship was teetering on the brink of collapse, and Harry's main concern was the effect that all this would have on Ella.

Ella came back into the kitchen, interrupting Harry's chain of thought. "Dad's taking me for a meal after school," she said with a happy smile on her face.

The prospect of a restaurant meal after school had swayed her. Harry wondered at the fickleness of people when they could be swayed by the offer of a free meal.

Ella said, "Oh my, look at the time. I'd better be off to school." She quickly gathered her things and stood near the door. "Sorry, Grandad, I'll have to leave my dishes."

He waived away the apology. "What else am I doing today? I have eight hours to wash dishes," he said in mocking self-pity.

She smiled at him. "I love you, Grandad."

It was an endearment that melted his heart every time. "I love you too, Tuppence," he replied.

Outside, a car horn sounded. "Mum's here," Ella called out and scurried out the front door. "See you later, Grandad."

"'Bye, Tuppence," said Harry as he watched her dash out the front door to her mother's car.

Ella jumped into the car and Harry waived at Katrina and he watched as they drove away down the street in the direction of the school. He went back into the house and washed the dishes. Some cursory tidying up had to be done to compensate for the residue of a distracted young person in the house and their belief that all chores were carried out by fairies while they were absent.

In an hour he was done. Outside, the weather remained fine and he decided to go for a walk through the park. He took with him his stock of stale bread to feed the ducks.

The park was in full bloom and teeming with screeching and singing birds. Insects hummed incessantly, busily fertilising plants or gathering pollen. Butterflies danced and darted about, constantly changing the patterns of coloured plants. The park carried a huge amount of civic pride, and rightly so. Its Victorian splendour had been restored by some European grant or other, but it was money well spent. It was one of the few things that the Council had got right.

Harry made his way to the lake and found the bench on the north-eastern tip that gave the best view of the park. It was sheltered by some well-tended bushes, so that when the sun shone it became the warmest part of the park. It was also where the swans and ducks gathered.

Harry's stock of bread was prolific. He had a friend at the bakery who gave him a regular supply of bread that had been removed from the shelves after it became unsellable. It took him a good fifteen minutes to get rid of it, and he made sure that every bird got something to eat.

"Morning, Harry."

It was a melodic voice with a hint of an Irish lilt. It came floating from behind a small copse on the shores of the lake about twenty yards to his left. It was Hazel, a woman who had become his friend in the last year or so. She was around forty-five years old with friendly green eyes and a quick smile. Despite being past her first flush of youth, she was what Harry would call buxom. Tiny flecks of white had invaded her copper hair and she had decided that she wasn't going to fight it by dying it. She wore a simple blue cardigan over a white top and blue skirt. She never wore trousers, thinking that they were unflattering and masculine.

That was one thing that Harry liked about her. He preferred women to be feminine, and to him that meant women wearing skirts and dresses.

"Morning, Hazel. It's a lovely day isn't it?"

Hazel sat down on the bench beside him and put her bag on the ground.

"It is, so why don't you tell your face that," she said. "It looks like you've lost a pound and found a sixpence."

Harry smiled. That was another thing he liked about her. She came straight to the point, but in a way that didn't upset you. Somehow there was a built in humour to her tone.

He considered his response. "I've not seen a sixpence for years," he said. "How are you?"

Hazel's reply was immediate and honest. "Much better than you by the look of it. Having a bad day are we?"

She shuffled along the bench next to him and patted his

32

thigh sympathetically.

Harry wasn't the type of person to unload his problems onto anyone else, or at least not the minutiae of domestic upheavals. His problems were his business.

"Family problems" he stated matter-of-factly.

Hazel nodded sagely and said, "Oh dear, those types of problems can be a right pain in the arse."

Harry laughed in spite of himself; Hazel's turn of phrase was typically apt. His normal restraint lapsed slightly. Hazel was a decent woman who wasn't prone to gossiping, so he volunteered more information.

"I think my daughter's heading for divorce. They're having a trial separation. They've got some difficulties." He resisted the temptation to use his fingers to draw quotation marks in the air.

"Oh dear," Hazel said. "Who's the one with the bit on the side then – him or her?"

Once again Hazel had come straight to the point. It was a question based solidly in the most common reason for wanting a divorce – adultery. Harry was about to explain what the difficulties were when he lost the ability to give a rational account of the situation. He exhaled deeply and said "There are faults on both sides."

Hazel raised her eyes to the heavens in disbelief.

Harry continued. "But I think my daughter is seeing someone else. I have no proof, just gut instinct."

He gazed at the far end of the lake where another man and woman had captured the attention of the ducks by feeding them more bread.

"Oh dear," Hazel said for the third time. "How's your granddaughter taking it?"

It was another incisive question. Harry considered his response. It was a question he found hard to answer. It was too soon really to judge. Her initial response had been predictable, but she'd borne the news quite well; only time would tell whether or not she'd endure the fallout of a broken marriage.

"It's hard to say," he replied honestly. "It was a shock to her, but we'll have to monitor the situation and act whenever possible to make sure things don't go pear shaped."

"You sound like the friggin' United Nations, Harry. Kids are more resilient than we give them credit for. This is part of the school for hard knocks, sure it is. With a little help, she'll get through it right enough."

Harry regarded his companion for several long moments, considering her remarks, before saying, "I'm sure you're right. It just doesn't make it any easier."

Hazel took hold of his hand and stood up.

"So then, Mister Harold Crimson, are you coming to my place or not? I've got a custard tart in the fridge just waiting for your choppers to get on the outside of it."

Harry held her hand tightly as he stood. "I might as well," he said. "I'm unlikely to get a better offer today." He smiled at her, with one eyebrow raised suggestively.

Hazel reciprocated.

"Oh, I don't know about that, Harry. We'll have to wait and see, won't we? C'mon, drag your arse this way."

Harry chuckled as she linked him and started walking. He allowed himself to be dragged through the park to the ornate gates guarding the exit.

***

It was around eight o'clock when he heard a car pull onto the drive. The engine remained running for a minute or so, then the vehicle reversed and sped away. The front door opened and Ella walked in wearing a face that suggested her restaurant meal had been consumed at a price.

"Have a good time?" Harry asked, rising from his chair and pecking her on the cheek.

She pulled a face. "Well, yes and no," she said. "Yes, I've been with Dad. I've eaten loads, and he even bought me a shandy. Wow! No, from the point of view that he was talking about Mum all the time and saying how she wasn't the woman he married and how she's let him down and rubbish like that. Do I really need to know all that? I don't think so. I'm going out with Mum tomorrow. I hope she doesn't do the same. I couldn't bear it. If they've got 'difficulties'," she raised her fingers and made the quotation mark signs that Harry had refused to use earlier in the day, "then let them sort things out as adults are supposed to. I'm not part of their problems; I'm a casualty of them. Sometimes adults can behave just like children. I'm just going upstairs to shower and change into my pyjamas."

She disappeared and bounded up the stairs two at a time.

Harry sat and pondered. Ella was right. Adults do sometimes behave like kids. He hoped that Katrina and Oliver weren't going to use Ella as an emotional pawn in the breakdown of their marriage. It was a fragile state of affairs and Ella's future was not part of their battleground. Perhaps Hazel was right. Kids were resilient. Perhaps it's the adults who can't cope very well.

***

After a couple of hours or so of watching television, Ella decided she was going to bed. It was Friday night and no doubt she had a full weekend of parental squabbles ahead of her.

"Are you going to finish off that story you started last night, Grandad?

"If you want me to," Harry replied thinking rapidly. "Get yourself upstairs and give me a shout when you're ready."

He watched her leave the room. She was a different girl to the one who'd stayed last night. He had expected a bit of see-sawing, emotionally, but she was acting as though everything was normal. Perhaps that was all part of it. What did he know?

Ella shouted. Harry went upstairs immediately.

"So where were we?" he asked in mock absentmindedness as he sat on the bed.

As quick as a flash she answered. "We had a woman who was happy, her husband and child, a magic mouse and a feller who had asked the woman to go away with him."

"Hmmm, ok, then. Let's see what happens next."

***

Inkarta went to see her friend Zelda.

Zelda was a very old woman who was also very wise, although she had a tendency to talk in mysterious riddles when she was counselling friends. She lived by herself in a cottage and made mosaics from pieces of tile and pottery. Her hands were skinny and hard, with long, thin, bony fingers. Her face was lined and wizened. She cackled like a witch, but she had a warm, soft heart. She carried a huge knitted bag wherever she went, which was full of things that everyone else needed.

Inkarta told Zelda about her frustrations surrounding Rivelo not spending enough time at the castle. She also told her that she thought she was being taken for granted.

Zelda had nodded sagely but hadn't judged Rivelo.

Neither had she endorsed Inkarta's point of view. Zelda saw things her own way, and she wasn't influenced by anyone. That was the reason Inkarta had come to see her.

"But I'm happy, Zelda," said Inkarta finishing off her cup of tea.

"Of course you are," said Zelda eyeing her suspiciously. "I can see the happiness oozing out of you."

"But I am," protested Inkarta.

Zelda peered into her face. "Say it again and you might start believing it. And what about Estraneo? How does he figure in all of this?"

Inkarta looked uncomfortable for the first time as she shifted her position on the chair.

"Estraneo? He's a nice man. Solid, reliable, dependable," she said. "Always on time. Always does what he says he's going to do. He has a wicked sense of humour and a quick wit. He's also very intelligent, gracious and ... "

"Sorry to interrupt, but I didn't want to know all that," said Zelda, her eyes narrowing, adding, with more than a hint of sarcasm, "So he's just an ordinary man."

"As I said, he's a nice man," retorted Inkarta defensively.

"And this nice man has asked you to go away with him next week, has he?

"In connection with work, obviously."

"Obviously," Zelda said.

"Rivelo is happy with it," Inkarta said.

"So you're going then?"

Inkarta said, "I suppose I am. Rivelo says it'll be a

valuable experience. I'll learn a lot."

"I'm sure you will," said Zelda drily. "What messages have been spelled out by the magic mouse in the room of tiles?"

"I have written them down, but they cannot be spoken."

Inkarta showed Zelda the messages.

Zelda nodded. "Remember this: Truth is stranger than fiction. If you go, then you'll know. Find your truth and you'll find out who the stranger in your life is."

Inkarta was confused. "What does that mean?" she asked.

Zelda smiled a knowing smile. "You'll find out soon enough," she said.

Inkarta went to the stall straight from Zelda's house. She thought long and hard about what Zelda had said and decided that it didn't make any sense.

Estraneo was waiting for her. He drew her to one side and said, "Are you coming with me next week?"

She smiled at him and said, "Yes."

He reached out and squeezed her hand. A look of absolute joy filled his face. He whistled a happy tune as he went about his business.

The day came when Inkarta said farewell to Rivelo and Lela and rode away in a carriage to a place deep inside the city. The city was teeming with people, but no-one seemed to notice Inkarta was there, except Estraneo. But she didn't mind that. It gave them time to be together. They went to a cottage, and Inkarta soon found herself in the arms of Estraneo.

They were deliriously happy.

On her way back to the castle, Inkarta was visited by dark thoughts. Remorse seeped into her soul and she broke down in floods of tears.

Estraneo tried to comfort her, but Inkarta rejected him.

"This can't continue," she said.

Estraneo was heartbroken. "Do you want me to go away?"

Inkarta said, "No, but I want you to stay away from me."

Inkarta told Rivelo that she wouldn't be going back to the stall because it wasn't really what she wanted to do.

Rivelo didn't mind that at all, even more so when Inkarta stopped complaining about him being away all the time.

Inkarta kept herself busy. On one or two occasions she disappeared into the room of tiles and wrote down some more messages spelled out by the magic mouse. However, after a couple of months had passed, Inkarta realised that she still wanted more out of life. The excitement she'd experienced when she was with Estraneo at the stall was missing. She realised that her life was colourless without it.

She went to see Zelda again and told her all that had happened, including the night in the cottage.

"So you found your truth, then," said Zelda.

"How do you mean?" asked Inkarta.

Zelda shook her head. "It's not for me to explain," she said. "It's for you to discover and realise the consequences."

Inkarta's brow furrowed, searching for meaning.

Zelda said, "Whatever will be, will be. Your destiny is not in your hands."

Inkarta said, "I blame Estraneo for all this. He

has confused me. I was happy until he came along. Now I'm not happy anymore."

Zelda said, *"If no-one changes, then there isn't a choice to make."*

Inkarta rode away from Zelda's house. She had some errands to see to in the village. Coincidentally, her route passed by Estraneo's stall. He was standing there. It was the first time they had seen each other for many, many days. Inkarta tried to be formal in her greeting, but within seconds she could not control her feelings and she rushed to embrace him. They kissed each other hungrily. They could not hide their feelings any longer.

Estraneo said, "Have you come back to me?"

Inkarta shook her head and said, "No. I have my own life to lead. I have Rivelo and Lela. They are my life. I need to have you in it, but not in the way you wish."

"So you are rejecting me again. At the same time you're asking me to hang around in case you change your mind. If that is the case, why am I confused by you greeting me like this?" said Estraneo.

Inkarta apologised. "I'm sorry, Estraneo. I'm confused. I love Rivelo and Lela. I also love you. I can't decide what I should do, so I'm staying with the life I have until the decision is made easier."

"How can that be?" he asked.

"I don't know," she said.

They separated, and, without speaking, Inkarta left, leaving a forlorn Estraneo next to his stall.

She left the sack containing the magic mouse behind.

***

"And that's it for now," Harry said. "Next instalment tomorrow, or whenever."

Ella was lying on her back staring blankly at the ceiling, a puzzled expression on her face.

"What're you thinking?" Harry asked.

"I'm trying to figure out what's going on. This isn't a typical fairy story, Grandad. It's complicated."

"Well, if you look at all stories there are plots and sub-plots. The characters may not be what they seem to be, or they might have different agendas. That's what drives the story along. You can accept it at face value or you can try to work out, like you said, what is actually going on. Tell me, Tuppence, what do you think is happening here?"

Ella considered for a long hard moment before answering, her left hand curling her hair in a clockwise demonstration of her thought processes.

"Well, I think that this Inkarta woman is married to one man, but has fallen in love with another one, and she's trying to come to terms with it. It's all a bit, sort of, old-fashioned type stuff, isn't it?"

"Falling in love isn't old-fashioned, Tuppence; it happens every day. There are rules, though. Society, or at least our society, only allows you to love one person at a time, in practical terms that is. The reality is that we are capable of loving lots of people."

Harry looked thoughtfully at Ella's face framed by the pillows and decided to continue.

"Now don't get me wrong. We love our parents, kids, our entire families and friends for that matter, in different ways, but that special someone floats our boat in ways you can't even imagine, yet. So imagine what it would be like to feel that way about two people at the same time."

"I know what you mean, Grandad. I love you in a different

way to Mum." Ella's expression didn't change. "But I've never been in love, so I can't say what I mean. It must be lovely."

Harry nodded. He was instantly taken back to a moment more than forty years ago when he'd proposed to Thelma. She'd mischievously said, "I'll think about it", but ten seconds later had said, "I've thought about it, and the answer's yes." Those ten seconds had been the longest of his life. Those ten seconds had taken him through a gamut of emotions from surprise and shock to despair, fear and, eventually, complete happiness. Being in love was more than lovely, it was absolutely marvellous.

"This Inkarta woman's got a problem, though, hasn't she," said Ella. "She likes the lifestyle her husband brings her; you know, the wonderful family life, but she likes having a bit on the side as well."

Harry's eyebrows shot up. It had been a while since he'd heard that expression, and he certainly didn't expect to hear it from his fifteen year old granddaughter, but it was an apt description.

"Well, yes, I suppose so," he said. "That's just one of the problems with loving two people. You want the best of both worlds."

Ella smiled at her grandfather squirming on the edge of the bed.

"You're not embarrassed, Grandad, are you?" she enquired cheekily.

"No, I'm not embarrassed," Harry said, "just a bit uncomfortable. I didn't think I would ever have this kind of conversation with my granddaughter. You should be talking to your mum or dad about things like this."

"I don't think that either of them are in the right frame of mind to discuss the meanings of your fairy stories, do you?"

It was a sarcastic retort that hit home to Harry. Perhaps

Ella wasn't as naive as he thought she was.

"Anyway," Ella continued, "Inkarta goes away with this man and has sex with him, then comes back home and continues as if nothing has happened. I don't like that. She's being dishonest. What does she think she's doing? What if her husband finds out? What about her daughter? And what's all this about a magic mouse that writes message on tiles? Anyway, I think she's being selfish. Somebody's going to get hurt."

Harry nodded again. "That may be so, Tuppence, but there may be other reasons why this has happened."

"Like what?" Ella asked. "Him being away from home all the time? I don't think so. It comes with the territory, doesn't it. You marry a rich, successful man and he has to spend time away from home. That's that. You can't have your cake and eat it. This Estraneo guy comes on the scene and gives her a little bit of attention and she's fallen into the trap. This guy's a stranger to her. It's wrong."

Harry got up off the bed and wandered over to the window. He peeked through the closed curtains before saying in a faraway voice, "You have to ask yourself who is the stranger in her relationships. Is Inkarta being taken for granted by Rivelo? There is a bigger question here: do you have to work at a relationship all the time?"

Ella considered that for a few moments before saying, "I don't know. But this story started off with Inkarta being happy and now she isn't. This Estraneo has spoilt it all."

"Has he?" Harry said. "Or has he shown her that there is a big wide world out there where she can be who she wants to be, a place where she can grow and be herself?"

"But she's already got a life, Grandad. What's that expression? Oh yes, you've made your bed so you can lie in it."

Harry shook his head. "That's not what I think. That's a

stupid saying. It means that if you've made a wrong decision, you have to take the consequences for life. You have to accept responsibility, that's true, but there is no reason to continue having a bad life just because of one mistake."

He thought for a moment then continued in a quieter voice. "Sometimes we make decisions based on very little information, or we think we have a free choice. Many times people find that their choice was limited by events or lack of information, and given different circumstances would have made different choices.

"But she has a husband and child. She has responsibilities," protested Ella.

"Yes, she has," agreed Harry. "I'm not trying to justify what she's doing. I'm trying to put forward another point of view. We're all so judgemental these days."

"Well, I don't think it's right," said Ella snuggling further down into the warm softness of her bed. "Even though she knows it's wrong, she continues doing it. And what's even more stupid is that she's told Estraneo that he's got no chance, but asks him to hang about anyway. That's taking the mickey."

"Well," Harry said while bending down and kissing Ella on the forehead, "that's enough for tonight. Goodnight, Tuppence."

He stood up, stretched and wandered to the door.

"Nite nite, Grandad. Will there be more tomorrow?"

"We'll see," Harry said, smiling. "I'll see you in the morning."

He closed the door behind him and went downstairs to the kitchen. He prepared a mug of hot milk before settling in his favourite armchair in front of the fire. His thoughts turned to Ella's day with her father and the impending day with her mother. He hoped a tug of love battle wasn't on the cards, but, as he had already acknowledged, adults adopted schoolyard tactics when their emotions were laid bare and their inadequacies were exposed. Ella wasn't past using one against the other to get her own way – a trait she had learned from her mother. She was her mother's child. His problem now was whether or not to act as Ella's guardian from the start, or to step in if required when, or if, problems presented themselves.

He deliberated well into the small hours as to what his role should be. He eventually decided to play it by ear, as he had always done in tricky situations in the past. He just wasn't sure if he was too close to everyone to be objective – and was objectivity required?

He went to bed, and for the second time in just over twenty four hours he felt his age.

4

Harry lay in bed. He usually greeted weekends the same way – a lie in until 7.30, followed by breakfast of a bacon sandwich and two mugs of tea while he caught up with the news on the radio. He'd had a disturbed sleep. More disturbed than the problems associated with his enlarged prostate usually caused him. Images and phantoms had visited during the night and made him restless and uncomfortable, confusing his body clock.

The first light of day was stealing through a gap in the curtains. The familiar quiet of dawn was broken only occasionally by a blackbird's song. His muscles were relaxed and pain free, until he moved to get up. He sat on the edge of the bed until gravity hauled everything into place, enabling him to stand and walk. He grabbed his dressing gown from the back of the door.

The stairs creaked as he made his way down to the kitchen. He convinced himself that the water in the kettle still had some heat left in it from the previous visit and made himself a mug of tea. He buttered three slices of toast and sat in his chair. During the night, he had decided to talk to Katrina. Just a general conversation, father to daughter, to see how the land lay. No hassle. No agenda.

Later, Ella got up, breakfasted and departed with her mother. Harry packed away the plates and gathered together the remnants of a loaf of bread. He regarded three quarters of a loaf in the bread bin on the brink of turning mouldy.

Since Thelma had died, his appetite had tapered off. Harry and Thelma had been inseparable since they'd married forty years ago, at the end of the 'swinging sixties'. Her passing, on their ruby anniversary, was a fitting tribute to her determination and strength of character. It was like the end of a contract, or reaching retirement. The date had become a target towards the end. His lounge had been a strange mixture of congratulations and sympathy cards until someone had taken them down one day when he went to buy a newspaper. The numbness in his brain wouldn't allow him to do it himself.

Feeding the ducks was one thing that Harry and Thelma had done for some time. The walk to the park was close enough to give them some exercise but not too far as to cause them problems. And the ducks were always grateful. He had kept up the habit when Thelma passed away. He didn't know whether it was duty or a reluctance to abandon simple pleasures that kept him going, but he continued in any case.

The park was also the place where he had first met Hazel.

As he left his house at the top of the cul-de-sac, he was aware of the curtain twitching neighbours who monitored his comings and goings. They had commiserated when Thelma died. Some even went to the trouble of preparing him meals, most of which ended up in the bin. However, when Hazel first appeared on the scene, there had been a sea-change in attitude, even though it had been three years since the funeral. The age old controversy of having a female friend and how that was construed caused him a great deal of irritation.

It was another sunny day. A Saturday. The weekend was

here and people milled around free from their daily grind. He smelled the bouquet of the flowers in the park long before he got there. The sound of a song thrush raised his spirits; it was a delightful sound.

He made his way to the lake, reached into his bag and tore the slices of bread. The ducks, swans and a fair sprinkling of pigeons and gulls jockeyed for position, eager to gulp down an easy meal. He toyed with them by pretending to throw, then not, and eventually scattering the bread in every direction. He poured the crumbs into the lake for the tiny fish. A few remnants of bread at his feet were scooped up and lofted into the air to be caught by the marauding seagulls. The daffy ducks randomly skimmed around the surface of the water like dodgem cars at a fair, antics that made Harry chuckle.

He stuffed the empty bag into his pocket and selected his favourite bench looking out over the lake. The birds flew away. The swans and ducks swam in all directions, their interest in him evaporating like an early mist in the sun. They knew that someone else would be along shortly and there'd be another free meal. They would perform their dance and get their reward.

The warmth of the sun was comforting. Harry closed his eyes and relaxed. His thoughts once again turned to the catalogue of events that had affected the lives of his loved ones. As he sat, he randomly sought pieces of information and incidents, and tried to link them together like some jigsaw of life. Some pieces fitted together immediately, but others, try as hard as he may, would not. He knew that unless he managed to fit everything together, the picture would not reveal itself, and understanding would be lost.

A voice interrupted his day dreaming.

"It's a sign of old age."

It was Hazel.

"Sleeping in the park, that is," she said.

Harry smiled without opening his eyes. "Ah, but it's worth it if I'm dreaming of you."

"Away with you, Harry Crimson, you smooth talker. There's no need to dream of someone if they're standing in front of you."

Harry opened his eyes. Hazel wore an emerald green dress – she rarely wore trousers as she thought they weren't feminine, and one thing she could not be accused of was not being feminine. "You look nice," he said.

"Nice, is it?" Hazel replied. "Didn't you know, Harry, that nice is one of those descriptions that can be regarded as an insult. It means something between presentable and shite, but you don't want to say so. So which is it?"

Suitably admonished, Harry said, "It means very nice." And he meant it. "In fact it means half way to wow! Are you off somewhere special?"

The perkiness evaporated instantly. Hazel smiled weakly. "Thanks, Harry." Her face crumpled into a frown and she lowered her voice conspiratorially, although there wasn't anyone within earshot. "I'm off to see Fino. There's a case review."

Fino was her husband's portmanteau name. His real name was Finbar O'Shea. The fusion of the first syllables of his first name and family name, with an Italian sounding pronunciation, was an endearment that only Hazel used.

Fino had been struck down with a form of dementia before his fortieth birthday and had rapidly deteriorated to the point where he was confined to a home. He didn't recognise Hazel when she visited him. They had been married less than five years and had no children. Neither Fino nor Hazel had any relatives; their parents having died back home in Ireland some years ago. Fino was two years older than Hazel.

A year or so ago, having consumed the best part of a bottle of champagne she had found at that back of her pantry

– bought for some long forgotten celebration – Hazel had told Harry that she'd been conceived in a chalet at Butlin's Holiday Camp, in Filey, where her mother had been a waitress. It had been her first job away from her domineering family in County Wicklow. Hazel's father had been a Redcoat named Jimmy, from Sunderland. His promises of everlasting love and vows of commitment hadn't lasted beyond the summer or the boundaries of North Yorkshire. Her mother had returned to Ireland, pregnant and in disgrace. She was quickly moved away from the area to have her baby. She never returned to her village. Hazel had made a fleeting visit there on holiday once and declared, "I'm glad I wasn't brought up in a dump like that."

Harry watched a cloud drift across the otherwise blue sky before turning his attention to Hazel. A similar cloud was visiting her face. "One of those days, then," he said.

"I guess so," Hazel replied. "Every now and then we sit round a table with a bunch of experts who tell me what they can't do. I wish someone would tell me what I can do. It tears me to pieces when they bring Fino in. He hasn't got a clue who *I* am, never mind *them*. He gets a bit agitated sometimes. The meeting usually ends with the experts expressing their sympathy and letting me go. It's so soul destroying."

Harry watched her closely. She had told him this many times now. He wondered whether there was any point in her going.

Hazel seemed to sense his question. "I keep going because I owe it to Fino. He's my husband and I love him dearly." Her voice broke and she choked back a few tears. "We had such great plans, we did."

Harry had never met Fino but knew all about him. He was suffering from frontotemporal dementia, a disorder that primarily affects the frontal and temporal lobes of the brain

— the areas generally associated with personality, behaviour and language. He had undergone dramatic changes in his personality, and displayed some socially inappropriate behaviour. He'd become impulsive and emotionally indifferent, had lost the ability to use and understand language and needed twenty-four hour care.

"Take the weight off your feet," Harry said gesturing towards the bench.

"I can't stay, Harry. I'm going to be late."

Harry shrugged. "Who's going to wag their finger at you?"

"I know what you're saying, but the sooner I get there and get it over with the sooner I can get the day over. I'm not at my best on days like this."

Harry looked hard into her eyes and saw the vulnerability working through her mind. He wanted to put his arms around her and give her a reassuring hug. Somehow, he thought she would welcome it, but he stopped himself. He didn't know what to do. He looked back across the lake and saw a solitary duck swimming towards them. He said, "I'm out of bread, Mistress Duck, come back tomorrow."

The duck seemed to hear what he said and veered off towards another woman, who was delving into a bag on the other side of the lake.

Hazel smiled. An awkward moment had passed. Harry was such a lovely man. "I'd better be off," she said as she got up and straightened her dress. "Will I see you tomorrow?"

Harry smiled warmly at her. "I hope so. Ella'll be at her mothers and I'll have most of the day free."

"I'm sorry, Harry. I never asked about what's going on in your world."

Harry waved his hand in dismissal. "Don't be sorry," he said. "There's nothing that can't wait. Oh, and if you need to, you know, talk about what happens at the meeting, then, you know my number. Give me a call. I'm in all night."

"Thanks, Harry."

"Good luck, Hazel. Take care."

She walked away towards the gates. It would take about fifteen minutes to walk to Sunnybrooks, the Home where Fino lived.

Harry watched until she disappeared from sight. Hazel was a good-looking woman who should've had a wonderful life with a husband, kids and a wide circle of friends. She deserved a normal life like anyone else, but there she was: existing on broken dreams and shattered promises, devoid of vitality, deprived of a meaningful and fulfilling life. He didn't pity her, but he felt very, very sorry for her.

With a heavy sigh Harry heaved himself upright and made his way back home. He collected a newspaper, fresh bread and milk on the way. Once home, he made a cup of tea and settled down to read the newspaper, savouring the peace and quiet.

***

Harry sat snoozing. The newspaper was spread on the floor where it had slid from his lap. His empty mug, emblazoned with 'World's Greatest Grandad', sat stone cold on the table beside his armchair.

Ella returned home noisily and bounded into the lounge. Harry woke with a start, involuntarily kicking the newspaper into greater disarray.

"Sleeping during the day are we?" said Ella, and then added mockingly, "that's definitely a grandad thing. Why do old people sleep during the day and then complain that they've had a bad night and never slept a wink?"

Harry rubbed his eyes. The almost sleepless twenty-four

hours preceding his nap would account for it. He yawned and stretched before saying, "It's a caveman thing. Human beings are designed to sleep twice a day. It makes us feel better and keeps us safe from sabre-toothed tigers." He picked up the newspaper and jiggled it into some semblance of order.

"We don't have sabre-toothed tigers anymore."

"Well, there you are then," said Harry. "It still works." He looked at his watch. "You're back early. How did things go with your mother?"

"A friend sent me a text asking me to go for a burger in town. I said to Mum that I'd like to go. She was a bit miffed because she'd scheduled the full day for me. But things were getting a bit heavy, talking about …" and here Ella mimicked her mother, "… 'the separation' and 'nobody knows what the future has in store for us'."

Harry frowned.

Ella carried on. "I know I have to talk about it to them, but I'm still not ready yet. It's too much to take all in one go. Can you have a word with her, Grandad? She dropped me off and went down to get you a custard slice from the cake shop. She'll be back in a minute."

The prospect of a custard slice raised Harry's spirits immediately. Then he considered Ella's plea. It was true that the whole thing had erupted in the last few days and it took a lot of getting used to. In Ella's eyes, she had gone from being a member of a loving nuclear family to being a disengaged teenager in a broken home. It wasn't surprising that she was reluctant to talk about the ramifications it would have for her future. Anyway, he needed to speak to Katrina and this was as good a time as any.

"Ok, Tuppence. I'll have a word, but you've got to get used to the idea sooner or later. It's not a nice situation to be in, but it's not in our control what happens. We just have to live with the consequences." He smiled. "If nothing else, I'll put on a little more weight," he said patting his paunch. "Off you go and I'll put the kettle on."

Ella ran upstairs and Harry strode into the kitchen.

"That'll be two cakes this week," he muttered. "Every cloud has a silver lining."

Katrina arrived just as the kettle was boiling. Ella ran downstairs wearing a coat and a fresh application of lipstick. She air-kissed her mother and Harry before rushing out.

Katrina said, "She's meeting some friends. I think there must be a boy involved somewhere."

Harry was making the tea and glanced up at her. "There's usually someone of the opposite sex involved somewhere along the line."

Katrina shot him a suspicious look. "What do you mean by that?" she asked.

"Just like I said. It doesn't matter what age you are. If you're attracted to someone then you're attracted to someone. Nobody can stop it. It's natural. But you can take steps to avoid it taking over your life."

Harry took the cakes out of the bag and put them down. His custard slice wobbled satisfyingly, while Katrina's jam doughnut relaxed, shedding tiny fragments of sugar on the tea plate. He carried the plates into the lounge and Katrina brought in the teas. Once settled, Harry bit into the cold, glutinous cake and savoured its flavour; eating a custard slice was like eating manna from Heaven. Katrina nibbled at her doughnut. An uncertain, troubled, look settled in around her, but Harry continued savouring his custard slice; any interruption to this sublime moment was indefensible.

Katrina knew her father well. She waited until the last few crumbs had been gathered and consumed before talking.

"Ella tells me you're telling her a fairy story at night. Don't you think she's a bit old for those now?"

"You're never too old to listen to a good yarn," Harry said putting his plate back onto the table and lifting up his tea.

Katrina shrugged. "I don't suppose it'll do her any harm. I just wondered whether she was trying to milk the situation a bit."

Harry looked her in the eyes, then spoke in a slow, almost menacing, tone to accentuate his words. "Katrina, Ella has been caught between the devil and the deep blue sea. Her world has fallen apart. It doesn't matter what you say to her; it's how she feels that counts. The two people who she's relied on all her life have, in her eyes, become selfish, petulant and angry. Everything she knows or understands about family life has become a lie to her. She feels safe here with me because I'm the same as I was last week, before all this blew up. Give her a bit of space. Cut her some slack. She'll adjust, but give her time. And tell Oliver that as well."

He sat back in the chair and steepled his fingers in front of his face. A flash of steely anger had come and gone.

Katrina looked at him for a long moment trying to work out if she'd been chastised. She quickly decided that all her father was doing was safeguarding Ella's interests. She softened immediately. "I'm sorry, Dad. I don't know what to do anymore. I'm trying to do what's best."

Harry flashed a disbelieving glance at Katrina. "What's best for Ella, or for you and Oliver?"

"For everyone, Dad. What do you want me to do? Do you want me to be unhappy? Do you really want that for me, Dad?"

Harry saw the beginnings of distress cloud her eyes. He reached across the table and gathered up his daughter's hands. He held them tightly.

"Of course not," he said. "If I knew what was best, I'd

tell you. I hate to see you like this, and I don't like to see Ella unhappy either, but it's got to be sorted and that means making some difficult decisions. You know what I say in times like this? Decide what you want and then try to make it happen. It doesn't do anyone any favours putting things off or letting things slide. That just causes conflict and indecision. Figure out what your priorities are and then go for it. You can evaluate and reconfigure your decisions as you go. You'll just keep mounting misery onto misery if you don't." He paused, then said, "Is there anything you want to tell me? Is there anything I need to know?"

He searched her face and saw her torment. He sensed the inner conflict. There was a battle going on inside, and whatever it was that was causing it won.

"I ... I ... don't know what you mean," Katrina stammered feebly. She lowered her eyes.

Harry now knew something was up and he felt an enormous void building between him and his daughter. He suddenly felt sad.

"Ok, love," he said softly. "Remember this. I've always said that you can't take on the world by yourself. I'm your dad. Whatever happens or has happened can't change that. As long as I'm alive I'll love you as much as I always have."

Katrina sobbed quietly, her head bowed. "I've got some issues to sort out. When I get my head together we can have a talk, yeah? Thanks, Dad." She got up and kissed the top of his head.

Harry felt as though he'd lost. His daughter didn't love him enough to trust him, unless, of course, she really was having great difficulties sorting out her head. Perhaps another opportunity would present itself shortly. He'd hate to think that communication between them had become stilted and fragmented.

"A friend of mine says 'If you bury your head in the sand it's only a matter of time before someone comes along and kicks you up the arse.'" He said it in a mock Irish accent and smiled at his daughter, who returned the smile through a veil of tears.

"I love you, Dad," she said as she left the room to cry in private and, eventually, to repair her make-up.

Harry found himself alone, damaged, deflated and drained of emotion. He picked up the jam doughnut, which had had one solitary bite taken out of it, and wrapped it in some kitchen tissue.

"That'll do for Mistress Duck and her friends," he muttered to himself.

5

Katrina sat in the conservatory of her detached four-bedroomed house on the outskirts of town. A desirable area to live, she would be the first to admit that, although not plush. If she could've afforded it at the time, the old village, half a mile away, would have been better, with its mature trees, manicured lawns and old buildings lending quality and refinement, as well as expense, to the area. Most of the houses in the village were well within the family purse strings now, but in the past few years she'd been less inclined to move there because it would have meant a different school for Ella. The village school was smaller and its results were inferior to Ella's current school.

She idly watched a goldfinch pecking away at something under the eaves of the house, although she was deep in thought. The weather outside had become overcast and dismal with isolated gaps in the grey skies affording sporadic glimpses of brightness. For many years she had taken advantage of days like this to weed the garden, deadhead the flowers, prune the hedges or cut the grass. However, her recent tardiness was evident. Even Oliver, who wasn't remotely interested in gardening, had commented that she'd lost interest in it, although that observation had come at the end of a tirade about her not caring about him, the house or their future together. To some extent that had been true. Recent events had consumed her thinking and focused attention on herself.

She was thinking about Ella and how she'd tried to tell her how she felt, and why she and Oliver had separated. She wasn't entirely satisfied with the result. In truth it had been the first time she'd actually verbalised her thoughts. She realised that it would've seemed entirely selfish, but that's how it was. She wanted to be recognised as Katrina. It didn't matter what her family name was, that only made her part of somebody else. She had her own identity and wanted people to know that. She wanted to make her own choices in life and decide her own future the way she wanted to, within her own time frame. However, no matter how many times she ran the arguments through her head she still came across as a selfish bitch, and it heaped huge amounts of guilt on her.

Her eyes were drawn to a wedding photograph on the sideboard. She had been a typical bride and the photograph captured the look of raw, unbridled love that she and Oliver had had. It'd been a perfect day, that one. She'd been with Oliver since leaving college and they'd spent a wonderful seven years together before deciding that marriage was the only option open to them if they wanted kids. She'd mistakenly thought that a little 'bundle of joy' would be a lovely addition to their perfect world. Reality had kicked in only when Ella was born. She was a screaming child who never settled, and the axis of the perfect world shifted, shimmied and shattered. For the next three years Katrina endured the hell of a crying child. At times she felt as though she couldn't cope. Her mother had offered to help but she was having her own problems due to menopause, which later resulted in a nervous breakdown. Her father had been a saint. He ran a business and looked after her mother as best he could, and still found time to help out Katrina with Ella.

Oliver had absented himself on several occasions, citing work as his excuse. It was an excuse that had permeated their marriage thereafter. She used to say to him, "When the going gets tough – you go to work."

His reply was always, "My work – our future."

For years he'd been proved right. Ella settled down and became a placid child who was outgoing and friendly. The family prospered and they'd made shrewd investments in property. It'd been a huge commitment, but it was well worth it. Oliver's promotions financed their lifestyle and Katrina played the parents' coffee morning game, followed by 'Ladies that Lunch' and other school related social fundraisers and fairs. She'd enjoyed it, in the main, but in the last couple of years she'd felt the need to do something else, although she had no idea what that might be.

Katrina walked over to the front window and looked along the street. It was quiet. This was a street where every man worked, and so did most women. Those who didn't were doing what Katrina did most of the time – shopping, cleaning and planning for their families. She wondered idly how many of them were happily married. How many of them had had a fling with someone else? Did any of them think or feel like her? She'd read magazines that suggested that the suburbs were rife with extra-marital liaisons and adulterous relationships. She reflected that life of that sort had largely passed her by.

When her friends had been sowing their wild oats in their teens and twenties, she'd been with Oliver. She'd looked at them and thought that they were looking for what she'd already had for years: a stable relationship with a lovely man who was good enough to be a fantastic husband and a wonderful father. She'd never considered the excitement of new relationships and sexual freedom as an end in itself. Many of her friends had married or were co-habiting, and some had divorced. One or two still tried to live the life they had set themselves nearly twenty years before. Until recently she'd pitied them. Now she saw them in a different light.

During one conversation with Emily, a friend from her college days, Emily had said that she'd made three lists and put everyone she knew in them. The first list was of friends like Katrina; the second list contained social friends, for nights out, meals, pictures and holidays; and the third list consisted of names who she could call for sex. Katrina had mentioned this to Oliver some time ago and he'd flirtatiously asked how he got a transfer from the first list to the third list. Katrina had, at first, been shocked with Emily, but she rationalised that in the context of organising your life, it made perfect sense, although she'd questioned what would happen in old age when the libido was lacking. Emily had simply replied, "Then I'll only need two lists."

Katrina wandered into the kitchen to wash her cup. She was suddenly overwhelmed by emotion and started to cry. What was she doing, she asked herself, as if she hadn't asked herself the same questions many times in the recent past. She slumped onto a kitchen stool and sobbed big shoulder jerking convulsions that were prefaced by a primeval wail. Something had to give soon, and she was frightened that she wouldn't come out of it in one piece when it was all over.

Her father knew there was something going on. She could tell by the way he raised his eyebrows and inclined his head to one side when he slowly and deliberately asked questions. He was a lovely man, an ideal dad. He wouldn't ask any specific, probing questions. He'd just create an explicit opportunity for someone to volunteer information, and then he'd listen. He'd done that all her life.

She'd tried to open up to him the other day. She wanted to tell him about her anguish and her anxieties. She wanted her dad to put his arms around her and take away her troubles like he'd always done, but she couldn't bring herself to tell him that she loved another man.

The phone rang. By the fourth ring she had wiped her eyes and steadied her voice enough to answer it in her usual bright style.

"It's me," said a baritone voice she instantly recognised as Will.

"Hi," she replied.

There was a pause.

Will detected a frostiness burning its way through the phone line. He said, "Is everything ok?"

"No," Katrina replied.

"Ok. We're having a bad day, right?"

Katrina sniffed.

"Is there anything I can do?" Will said, knowing the answer.

"Yes. You can get out of my life and leave me alone. Why can't you just be my friend like you used to?"

Will sighed and put forward his usual argument. "Katrina, I love you, and I know you love me. I want to be with you all the time. I want to marry you. Just say the word and I'll be there. One day we'll have to tell the world how we feel about each other, and the sooner the better as far as I'm concerned."

"It's not as simple as that. I've got Ella, Oliver and Dad to consider."

"And I'm not sacrificing anything? Is that what you're saying? I've got family too."

Katrina closed her eyes replaying images from the last few months in her mind.

Will still lived with his wife in the marital home. When Katrina first met him he had been remote, stand-offish even, but that self-imposed emotional isolation had quickly evaporated when they were together. It soon became evident to everyone that there was a spark between them. Within a few weeks they'd experienced that special frisson reserved for potential lovers, and Katrina had populated her diary with meetings and shifts in the charity shop to coincide with Will's time there. Engineering time together was easy; Oliver was more relaxed because Katrina wasn't on his back all the time and Ella was at school, doing homework or with friends. An extra bit of planning was all that was needed.

Katrina knew he was right, but it created so many problems.

"I'm sorry, Will. I know you're giving up your life as well. I just think it's so much easier for you."

"Easier? Perhaps. My kids are older than Ella, and they're away from home, so in that respect it's easier; and my parents are dead, so I have nobody to answer to there; and I've already been through the bad part with my wife at another time, but it's never easy for anybody concerned. I see my future with you and I'm trying to make that happen."

"I know, but can it ever happen? We've both got so much to lose."

"And so much more to gain," Will said. He paused and in a quiet, subdued voice said, "You've sent me away a dozen times, Katrina, and each time you've broken off a little piece of my heart. It can't take much more. If you send me away this time, I don't think I'll ever be able to come back. Just give me the chance to love you forever."

"I've left him, Will. We've separated."

Will was shocked by the suddenness of that statement. It took him a few moments to regain his composure. He drew a deep breath, giving him time to formulate a response. This was a crucial point. He didn't want to blow it all to hell.

"Wow," was all he could manage. Then, "How's Ella?"

Katrina was taken aback. She'd expected him to say something like 'it's about time' or 'when are you getting divorced?' She didn't expect him to enquire about Ella. But that was him, wasn't it? He was a kind, thoughtful guy. He had the same family values as she did, even if they were both prepared to break up their own families to be together.

"She's as well as can be expected given the circumstances. She's staying at Dad's until things quieten down. Dad's feeling a bit confused. I think he knows there's something going on. I'll have to tell him about us soon."

"So there is still an 'us' then?" Will said in as gentle a voice as he could muster. "In the long term, I mean."

There was a brief silence before Katrina replied. "Don't rush me, Will. I need to take my time on this. I want to make sure that what I'm doing is the right thing."

"You have all the time in the world, Katrina. I won't rush you. I just need to know that we'll be together someday. That'll keep me going forever and a day. I love you."

Katrina could feel herself about to break down again.

"I have to go," she said hurriedly.

She put the phone down and then crumpled into an armchair.

***

Will held the phone for some time before returning it to its cradle. He leaned back and reflected on his relationship with Katrina. He loved her dearly and wanted to marry her. And, yes, of course, other people were involved, so things couldn't happen at once. Incremental changes were what was required, that would minimise the impact on their lives, but he was beginning to think that maybe there should be one almighty rift to start the ball rolling.

He'd tried all ways to get Katrina to make the break from Oliver. She seemed to think that getting a divorce from him meant divorcing her whole family – and she wouldn't do that. Her family meant everything to her, hence her many attempts to exile him from her life in the hope he'd lose interest in her. The opposite had happened. Each break up had made him more steadfast in his resolve to overcome any obstacle she could manufacture and place between them. He knew she loved him, but was it enough?

Katrina and Oliver had separated. That was the first step. If this was indeed true, there were a few other substantial problems to overcome. Katrina had told him about the accusations made by Oliver that 'she'd had an affair with Will'. She'd also told him how her father had made a secret visit to the shop to find out who Will was. He'd laughed. The shop that day had been staffed by William, another volunteer. Katrina hadn't quite qualified that for her father because it appeared to make him happier. She hadn't told him that her Will was out at that time.

Will blinked back a tear and composed himself. There wasn't much he could do to help the situation along. All he could do was encourage and support Katrina in her decisions, and to be there for her after she'd made them.

***

Oliver sat at his desk and wrangled with his diary, trying to fit in a meeting in Manchester. He'd all the time in the world now that he was, in essence, a free man. He didn't have to drive back home immediately. In fact, he didn't need to drive home at all if he didn't want to.

He spent a few moments considering his options, and the possibilities ended in wild fantasies of debauched nights in some extravagant hotel room, a career of random pick-ups and a playboy lifestyle. Then reality came back to haunt him.

He sighed forlornly. None of this was his fault. All he was trying to do was make his way in the world and provide for his family. He had married a wonderful woman who had given him a beautiful daughter. He'd worked hard at his career, maybe doing an extra mile too many sometimes, but only because he wanted to be the best in the business. It had worked. Although he wasn't the most intelligent, or gifted, member of staff, he'd been promoted steadily through the company to a senior position in management. He was earning big money now. And he was still ambitious. He would agree that once or twice, or maybe more than that, he'd had to cancel family outings or dinner dates to accommodate his work ethic, but that was acceptable on the ladder to success, wasn't it? Something had to give.

He shook his head ruefully. Something gave alright – his marriage. He'd been sick of Katrina harping on about him being at work, and was glad when she found something to occupy her time. A couple of times he'd been frustrated when he'd had to rearrange work so she could go to some stupid conference somewhere to talk about shop work, charities, teams or something equally as trivial. And now she'd taken up with another man, or so it seemed.

Despite his situation Oliver smiled. 'Taken up' was an expression his mother had used. He could see in his mind's eye the expression of contempt and disdain she wore when using that phrase. He never thought he'd be using the same expression to describe something feeding his own wife had done. He didn't deserve to be treated this way. None of this was down to him.

The diary was still in his hand. He needed some time off to sort his head out. He leafed through the pages and found that the next convenient day to have off was three weeks hence. He couldn't possibly be away from work during that time; there were too many appointments that needed his personal attention. Nobody else could do what he did.

He put the diary back onto the desk. The work would keep him busy and take his mind off things. As long as Ella was ok, then so was he. If Katrina decided to take a fancy man, another one of his mother's expressions, then so be it. His conscience was clear. He was the victim in all this.

Oliver stood up and looked out of the office window. It was nearly dark. Everyone else had long since gone home. He decided to call into the pub on the way home. A couple of beers, a gammon steak with chips, and a bowl of apple crumble would ease the pain. He turned the lights off, secured the premises and walked to the car he had left in the car park thirteen hours before.

He tasted his first beer ten minutes later.

6

Katrina woke to rays of sunshine streaming through her blinds as if they were a metaphor for her own mental state. Her thoughts had cleared, and everything that had to be said lay before her with astonishing clarity. It was a moment of epiphany. With remarkable calmness she rang the charity office and told them she wouldn't be in today. Will would hear of it immediately and be seized with dread, but that wasn't her problem. She needed to be straight with people, especially her dad. She couldn't tell Ella yet; it was still too raw for her to handle. First thing's first.

She drove to her father's house and parked in the drive. Her resolve evaporated slightly as she got out of the car, but she quickly garnered herself for the conversation she was about to have. The front door opened before she had knocked on it.

Harry was curious. It was unusual for his daughter to call on him mid-morning. Was this another chapter to her haphazard and, frankly, exhausting story? What was the matter now?

"Come in, love," he said in his usual light-hearted tone. Might as well start upbeat, he thought. "Kettle's boiled."

Katrina went straight into the lounge and sat on the edge of the sofa.

Harry took his time to make the tea, reflecting that it seemed his life was turning into a series of tea parties, although no-one appeared to be enjoying them. He entered the room to find Katrina dabbing a tear from the corner of her eye. Harry braced himself and sat down. "I don't suppose you're here to tell me good news then?" he asked.

Katrina whimpered, then melted into a flow of tears. "Oh, Dad, it's such a mess."

Harry got up and did what dads do. He held Katrina close as she lost control, saying nothing. There was nothing to say. He was a father caring for a daughter who was distressed. It didn't matter how old you were, it was the relationship that counted. He recalled many moments when he had done exactly this – comforted his distressed daughter. Whatever had sparked the tears on this occasion had been lost in the reparation of her mind and soul. It didn't matter anymore. Whatever had happened could be mitigated or repaired without judgements being made.

The sobbing ceased, but Katrina hung on desperately. Harry waited. He would let her respond in her own time.

Katrina felt her father's heart pounding inside his chest; a steady, rhythmic, reassuring beat that reflected his position in her life. He was a rock, always there, a beacon of light in the gloom and murk that had surrounded her at various times over the last forty years. Why she had ever kept anything from him seemed totally stupid now. When had he ever not offered help, guidance or advice? Never, was the answer.

"Dad," she said in a voice that sounded just like Ella's when she was upset, "I'm having an affair."

There was no reaction from her father. At first she wondered whether he had heard her. She lifted her head from his chest and looked into his moist eyes. He still didn't say anything.

"I'm having …" she started, repeating what she had said, but her father interrupted her.

"I heard you, love," he said gently. "Dear, oh dear, oh dear."

Katrina was shaking. She sat down on the sofa. Her father sat next to her, holding her hand. For the next hour she told him the story, trying desperately to be objective about it. She knew that if she tried to justify her actions her dad would see right through it.

Most of what she told him, Harry had already guessed, and all those apparently incongruous events of the recent past began to fit smoothly into his understanding of his daughter's strange behaviour. He brushed away conversation about the frequency of sexual encounters with a shake of the head. "That's irrelevant," he said. "Whether it's one time or a hundred and one times doesn't matter. Sex occurs in the head long before it reaches below the waist. At some stage you decide yes or no. Once the decision is made, you can't go back."

When she was through, Harry asked, "How much of this does Oliver know?"

Katrina pulled a face. "Not many facts, but he's not stupid, Dad. He's joined all the dots and has a good idea of what's going on."

"And what about Ella?"

"She knows nothing. I've asked Oliver not to tell her anything and he's agreed, but I don't know how long that'll last. You know what he's like; he can blow up at any time."

"I don't blame him on this occasion," Harry said. "His wife is having an affair with another man. I think he's allowed to be a bit annoyed."

It was an admonishment, a small one, but an admonishment nonetheless.

"I'm not judging you, Katrina, but you have to see things

from his point of view as well as your own. It's only then that you can rationalise his actions. If his world has fallen apart then it's only natural that he fights back, or at least tries to destroy the world of those who destroyed his. When you make decisions, put yourself in the other person's shoes and try to imagine what they're thinking. It sometimes makes it easier if you can empathise in some small way."

There was a brief moment of silence while they reviewed and collected their personal thoughts.

"There's something else," Katrina said slowly and deliberately.

Harry raised an eyebrow. What on earth could be as serious as this, he thought.

"Go on," he said.

"It's about Will."

"He's married as well, is he?"

She became slightly agitated and started wringing her hands. "Yes, he is."

Harry lounged back in the chair and puffed out his cheeks. "You don't do things by halves, love, do you? That makes it a bit more complicated."

"Please don't hate him, Dad."

He glared at her. "You know me better than that," he said. "I measure a person by their actions and who they are, not by what they are. But, let's not hide from the fact that others will judge you. As far as they're concerned you're a married woman with a family and he's a married man with his own family?" He raised his eyebrows to ask her to verify the statement.

She nodded.

"They will say that there are now two broken families. And it's all your fault. You can't rationalise with prejudice."

"I love him," she said simply.

It was the first time she had said so to anyone out loud. The weight of that statement seemed to crush her and, curiously, to also give her strength. The clarity of this morning's thoughts revisited her, as she looked deeply into her father's eyes for solace.

"Help me, Dad. I need advice, more so now than I've ever needed in the past."

Harry took both her hands. "Now, how do we handle things in our family," he asked, before answering it himself. "We ask ourselves what we truly want and then try to make it happen. I have to admit that everything is not within our control, but we'll work through it."

Katrina noted the use of we and our. This was a joint venture now. She wasn't alone anymore.

They had lunch. Harry made a ham sandwich and they shared a packet of crisps, washed down with a cup of decaffeinated coffee. The gloom lifted. There was a problem that had to be solved and they set about talking through the options. Did she have to make a clean break of things? When did she tell Oliver and Ella the truth? Did they even have to do that? Did she need to see a solicitor? Harry even asked if Will felt the same about her. What was the likelihood of his wife causing problems?

Harry was ever the pragmatist. He made a to-do list and then prioritised them for her. Top of the list was how matters could be dealt with without causing undue pain to Ella.

"The recriminations of separation and divorce are life changing," he told her. "People, especially kids, are resilient, but they still bear the emotional scars even into their adult lives. Their future relationships are moulded by their experiences, and in many cases that can be devastating. It's all well and good to make lists, but to carry them out is a different matter altogether."

7

It was after ten o'clock when Ella arrived back from her friend's house. Harry didn't approve of the time, especially when she had school the next day, but she had her mother's permission and that was the end of that. He thought it was one of the concessions her mother had made to her in appeasement – one of the many, he told himself.

"You'd better get upstairs and ready for bed," he said to her. "I'll bring your drink up for you."

"Thanks, Grandad," she said guiltily, and ran up the stairs two at a time and went straight into the bathroom.

A little later, her voice sailed down to Harry, who had gone into the kitchen to boil the kettle.

"Grandad, are you going to finish off that story you started telling me?"

"Oh, ok, I may get it finished tonight."

It was a simple statement but it showed that he had as much resolve as his daughter when it came to denying Ella.

He took a few minutes to let his mind wander through the tale he had told so far. It had been a rough outline of what he thought was happening with Katrina, his way of weaving bits of information, speculation and fantasy together to make sense of it all. He made mental notes on how it should progress, although he found himself wondering what should, or what shouldn't, be included.

By the time the hot drinks were ready, he knew what to say. He had to carry on as before and make the story run parallel to real events. It was a challenge to do that while maintaining the structure of a fairy tale.

He carried the tray up to Ella's room shouting, "Knock, knock" before reaching the bedroom.

"Come in, Grandad. I'm in bed."

Ella was in her red tartan pyjamas. He put the tray on the bedside table and pointed to her cup. He picked up his own and slurped a theatrical mouthful before smacking his lips.

"Now where were we?" he exclaimed conspiratorially.

Ella rolled her eyes. "We have a bored woman who's confused because she loves two men. Her husband is always working and another man has paid her a bit of attention and it's turned her head," she said mockingly.

Harry smiled. "Well, that's trivialising things a bit, but you're probably right. She probably thinks she's being taken for granted by her husband, and Estraneo has given her a little bit excitement."

"Oh, I think it's more than a little bit excitement he's giving her," Ella said with a wink and a laugh.

Harry was shocked. "Ella! Don't be so coarse."

"I'm sorry, Grandad," she said grinning. "I couldn't resist it."

Harry was a bit nonplussed to hear his granddaughter come out with innuendo like that. If someone else had said it he would probably have smiled and nodded in agreement, but, coming from Ella, it proved that the girl was growing up quickly. Time was moving on, and the innocence of her youth had crumbled like a battered limestone pillar in stormy seas.

"Ok. Let's see what happens next," Harry said.

***

Inkarta was having a bad day.

After Lela had gone out to stay with a friend, she approached Rivelo and said, "I'm unhappy about our situation together. I feel disconnected from you, and although we live as a family, we aren't one anymore."

Rivelo shrugged. "Tell me what's wrong and I'll see what I can do."

Inkarta told him again about her dissatisfaction; about how awful it was that he was away from home for long hours and how it impacted on their family life, and how they were unable to go anywhere for any length of time because of Rivelo's roaming. She also said that they hadn't been acting as man and wife for some time.

Rivelo loved the work he did. He loved Lela and Inkarta, but he was doing what he had always wanted to do, and he was respected because of it. He side-stepped the problem and hoped the moment would pass. One day Inkarta would praise him for sticking to his guns. He was building assets for the future. Their future.

Inkarta reluctantly acknowledged that Rivelo wasn't going to change as he kissed her goodbye and went away again. Today he was going further away and wouldn't be back until tomorrow.

Later that day, Estraneo decided to return some things to Inkarta that had been left by her some weeks ago. He had forgotten to give them to her the last time they had met at the stall. As he approached Inkarta's castle he heard her singing. Her voice was coming from an area at the back of the castle, near the swimming pool. He walked around the back and saw Inkarta lying in the sun. He listened to her beautiful, soft singing voice.

She only noticed him when he was so close that he stood over her.

"I've come to return some things you'd left at the stall," Estraneo said. He hesitated a moment and added, "I've also decided to stick around, in case you change your mind. You know that my dream is to make you my wife someday. I can't do that if I am not here to make it happen. Although I don't like the conditions you place on our meetings, I'm willing to try them."

Tears ran from Inkarta's eyes. "I'm sorry for asking you to do that," she said, "but I've got enough trouble without losing you as well."

She stood and kissed him. Their passion was immediate and intense. She took his hand and led him into the castle.

A new understanding grew between them, and over the next few weeks, Inkarta met Estraneo on several occasions. They settled into a new routine, and Inkarta soon became two separate people – the woman who was friend and lover to a new partner, and the loving wife and mother to her family.

Rivelo and Lela welcomed the old ways. However, Rivelo knew it was only a matter of time before his wife became unhappy again. She was a difficult woman to please. And he was right. The two worlds Inkarta occupied became a heavy burden for her to bear. Without warning, she went away to a secret castle to think about her problems. After a few days, she returned to see Rivelo and Lela.

They were glad she was home and family life

returned to normal.

Rivelo said, "Now that you're here I can go back to what I was doing before you disappeared."

He rode away.

Lela said, "I've made arrangements to stay at a friend's house. My father said I could go."

Lela went out.

Inkarta made her way to Estraneo's house. He welcomed her and invited her in, but she declined.

She said, "I'm sorry Estraneo, but we can never be together."

"I can't live without you," he said.

"You must," she said. "You must choose to move away and forget me."

"I can never forget you," he said.

Inkarta hurried away sobbing. Estraneo stood at his door and watched his future disappear into the dusk.

***

"So that's the end?" enquired a surprised Ella.

"It might be," Harry said. "Something else might happen to make the story longer."

"Like what?" she asked innocently.

Harry stared into the recesses of his mind before answering. "I don't know. In fairy stories anything can happen."

"It's not a very good story, is it? It looks like everybody lost out in that one. Whatever happened to a happy ending? What happened to the magic mouse? Did it just get left on the stall? What were the messages that she wrote down?"

"I don't know," Harry said, perhaps the mouse ran away when the sack was left out. Nobody would've seen it because it disappeared in sunlight. The messages couldn't be said in any case."

Ella pulled the duvet over her and snuggled down. "Not one of your best, Grandad."

"You win some, you lose some," Harry said. He knew she was right. The story was a stinker. He'd been careful to navigate between what he knew and what he had speculated on. He had fallen short on both counts. It wasn't real enough and it wasn't fantastic enough to be a viable fairy tale. "Fairy stories reflect life to a great extent. Does everything have a happy ending? I don't think so. We can all have happy times, but they don't last forever."

He paused a moment, searching for an example to illustrate the point. He didn't have to look very far.

"I had your grandmother. We had a good life, then she died. At the time I didn't want to carry on. I didn't think I would laugh again. People used to say 'You've got family to help you'. They were right, but your grandmother meant more than that. She was my friend, my companion and ..." he coughed, "... my lover."

Ella listened intently. There was something important being said.

Harry continued. "She used to look after me. She was always there. Sometimes I would reach out and touch her hand, and she would hold me. And there were times when she lay next to me in bed and just looked at me with her lovely blue eyes. It was the most marvellous feeling in the world. It was a look that told me she loved me. It's an incredible feeling, Ella, knowing you are loved."

Harry stared at nothing in particular, his memories washing over him. He felt Ella's hand on his cheek as she brushed away the tear that had stolen down his face.

"I miss her so much," he said quietly.

Ella sat up and hugged him.

They sat for a few long moments comforting each other, not saying a word.

"Love is such a wonderful feeling. The most powerful feeling in the world," Harry said as he dabbed his eyes with a tissue from the box next to Ella's bed, "but it can tear you apart when it's gone, or is taken from you. Remember that, Ella."

He picked up the tray and cups and stood, looking at Ella, assessing her emotional state. Her eyes were damp. He wondered if he should stick around for a few minutes to make sure she was alright, but she seemed thoughtful rather than distressed so he said, "Nite nite, Tuppence," and left the room.

Ella didn't say a word.

Harry was unsure whether or not she had heard him. He went downstairs and washed up, and then sat in his chair admonishing himself for getting upset; not that he wasn't ashamed of showing Ella his emotional side, but she had a lot going on at the moment and he didn't want to add to her burden.

After half an hour he locked up, turned out the lights and went up the stairs. He paused briefly outside Ella's room and listened. He didn't hear anything, assumed she was asleep and went to bed.

***

Ella lay awake. She heard her grandfather come upstairs and saw his shadow underneath the door as he waited a few seconds. She hadn't realised that her grandad still got upset about her grandma. It'd been a few years now and she wondered why he hadn't got over it. Perhaps he never would.

She felt a bit uncomfortable about her grandad crying in

front of her, but it had been so natural, and, after a moment, a warm feeling engulfed her. They had shared something special just then. For some reason she felt closer to him. She didn't think that was possible as she loved him so very much anyway. It made her feel curiously mature. She turned over and tried to sleep, but the chaos of her life intervened time and time again. She mulled over the fairy story and started to rationalise the emotional entanglements there. In a state of half sleep, the story and real life intermingled and became one and the same, and neither appeared to have a solution.

8

Harry stared out of the window at the sky.

He had arranged to see Hazel. He was interested in what had happened at the Home with Fino. She'd rang him when she'd returned from the meeting, clearly upset, but had refused his offer of a listening ear.

The sudden movement of a bird attracted him from his reverie – a white blackbird. A white blackbird, he'd thought months ago. It had sent him scurrying to the internet to find out what would cause such a thing; he had found the word leucism, a pigmentation issue in the genes.

Two squabbling male blackbirds competed for the attention of the leucistic bird, which sat, apparently unconcerned, on the fence waiting to be claimed. Below her, newly hatched starlings worried an empty seed ball net – its first forlorn attempt at foraging.

Harry had noticed, earlier, that Ella had been subdued at breakfast. She hadn't said much, but she had taken time to smooth his hair and straighten the collar on his shirt. He hadn't said much either. There was vulnerability in the air that bordered on embarrassment. It was a strange situation that tested both of them. She had hugged him – or, more correctly, had attached herself to him – when she'd left for school, but without making eye contact. Perhaps she wasn't dealing with her feelings today. Whatever the case, Harry went with the flow and said goodbye as normal.

***

It was overcast and dull, although it wasn't raining. Harry walked briskly through the park, stopping briefly near the lake to dispose of Katrina's doughnut. Mistress Duck quacked her way to the front of the queue and confronted anything that tried to invade her domain. Harry was her provider.

He reached Hazel's house and stood at the end of the drive to admire its Victorian facade. It was a detached house with a solid feel to it. Its large windows and substantial wooden door gave it a gravitas that declared its self-evident majesty to the neighbourhood.

Hazel answered the door. She wore little make-up and a floral kaftan splashed with burnt orange flecks that strangely complimented the colour of her hair. "Come on in, Harry," she said. "Make your way through to the kitchen. The kettle's boiling its arse off and me scones are still warm."

Harry smiled at the comment and laid his coat over the back of a chair. He sat next to the stove. The smell was delicious. He hadn't had homemade scones in years.

Hazel prattled on about anything and everything as she busied herself assembling a tray, jam, butter, double cream, cutlery, plates and serviettes before pouring a real cup of tea through a strainer. The scones were firm but light, liberally laced with sultanas. By the time the butter, jam and cream had been added, the scone was a meal in itself.

Harry ate two before sitting back in the chair with a fresh cup of tea. "That was delicious," he said with a great deal of satisfaction.

"You're only saying that because it's true," Hazel replied. "I'm a good home cook, even if I say so myself. Nothing fancy, mind you, but all the traditional home cooking, like your roast dinners, stews, cakes, bread and stuff like that, then I'm the one to beat."

"I'm not arguing," Harry said. "The evidence has been consumed."

"Not all of it," Hazel replied. "I've put a couple away for you to take home. Eat them within two days, mind you, or they'll end up being fed to that fat bird in the park. And I'm not talking about the woman who runs the caff."

Harry chuckled. Hazel never failed to lift his spirits despite, in his view, her desperate upbringing and married life.

"You look a bit troubled, Harry."

Harry sighed. He didn't know where to start. He hadn't come to unburden himself, though he couldn't think of anyone else who would be better at listening than Hazel. But he also knew that Hazel's problems were still unaddressed.

"Let's hear about your day at the Home first, then I'll tell you about mine. How's Fino?"

Her eyes darted around the room as she gathered information from files stored in her head. She selected the relevant facts and sucked out the emotion before fixing her gaze on Harry.

"There's no simpler way to say it, Harry. Fino's dying. He'll be gone shortly." Her tone was almost matter-of-fact.

For an instant, Harry thought she was joking, but his confusion gave way to shock. "Dying? How?" was all he could muster.

Hazel stood up, walked over to a mahogany dresser and picked up a letter. "When I went to the review the other day they told me that Fino was deteriorating more rapidly than they had ever experienced, and if that rate continued he would be dead within weeks, maybe even days. They wrote it down for me."

She handed Harry the letter.

Harry read through it. It was full of medical terminology and littered with probably and possibly, but the prognosis was that Finbar O'Shea was not long for this world.

"Wow," said Harry. "I'm so sorry, Hazel. If there's …" his words trailed off as he realised that a hundred and one other people would say those words. "Hazel, I'm here for you."

"Thanks, Harry. I might want one of your famous cuddles sometime."

"Anytime," he said.

Hazel stared at him for a long moment then said in as timid a voice as he had ever heard from her, "Harry, can I have one now?" She collapsed into Harry's arms and wailed mournfully.

Harry held her tightly, his memories jostling for position, stirring emotions, threatening to spill out into the mid-morning gloom. He let it flow through him. "Oh God Almighty!" he said. His voice cracked and they were both consumed by their fears and uncertainty.

They hung onto each other without saying a word for a long time before they broke off. A new calmness settled in between them; they were now more than two friends sharing a laugh, a cake or feeding the ducks in the park. There was closeness, intimacy; they'd shared a moment of supreme revelation normally reserved for partners. A touch of the hand was now expected, rather than unusual. There was a mutually reassuring safety between them, and both were comfortable with it.

"Thanks, Harry. I needed that."

"You don't have to thank me, Hazel. I had some things in my head that I needed to get rid of as well. We both needed it

… we'll probably need it again in the future."

Hazel slowly nodded and dabbed at her red-rimmed and puffy eyes with a tissue. "I don't know what to do next," she said.

"There's nothing to do except get on with your life and wait for the inevitable. With Fino … it'll happen soon enough. Is there anybody to tell?" Harry asked, knowing the answer.

"There's only me," Hazel whispered. She got up and put the letter on the dresser, stopping to look at herself in the mirror. "Oh my God, look at my face." She dropped her chin onto her chest and took a deep breath before looking at her image again. "I'm not as young as I was. It takes longer to recover the older you get." She returned to the sofa and sat next to Harry. "To be honest, Harry, I've been a widow for years. Ever since Fino went into that place I've been by myself. And now, when the time is coming when I'll be a real widow, I haven't the foggiest idea what to do."

Harry reached out for her hand, like he'd done to Katrina only a day or so before. Hazel grabbed it eagerly and held on.

"You're a dear friend, Hazel. I can only offer to help you in any way I can." Harry bent over and kissed her on the forehead. "C'mon, put your happy face on and I'll take you for lunch."

She hesitated, but Harry put his arm around her shoulder and said, "The situation today is the same as it was yesterday. Life goes on. You can go with it, or against it, but you can't sit around and do nothing. Now dry your eyes and get your coat."

Hazel nodded and went to ready herself. At times like this you had to rely on the good advice of a dear friend rather than back your own judgement.

They ended up in the café in the park, after deciding not to eat Italian; after the scones, Harry didn't have much room for anything else. Hazel wasn't hungry either so they shared a toasted teacake with cinnamon butter and a pot of tea.

The dark clouds had lifted and shafts of brilliant sunshine broke through. People scurried around living their lives and worrying about their problems. The lunchtime crowd filled the room.

"The maternity leave mob," Harry joked. "Their prams long since discarded."

Hazel laughed at that. "So what's happening in your world?" she said, stirring the pot of tea ready to pour.

Harry sat back and puffed out his cheeks. After that morning's closeness with Hazel he felt confident enough to throw off any semblance of embarrassment about having a dysfunctional family and told her everything. He spoke at length about Katrina's affair with Will and the separation it had caused, and about Ella staying with him for the time being.

During Harry's monologue Hazel had finished her tea and reordered another pot, and when a suitable break presented itself she excused herself and went to the toilet. She came back after a few minutes and sat down opposite him.

"You've been a busy little bee," she said. "The last thing you needed was me dumping more stuff on you."

"No, Hazel. Your stuff puts my stuff into perspective."

"How're you going to tell Ella?" she asked. "Although it's not your job to do that, you know."

"Katrina can't do it; she's too emotional at the moment. Oliver is too angry. There's only me left. Ella trusts me."

"You're putting yourself into a hell of a situation, Harry. It might blow up in your face if you're not careful."

"I've already started to tell her, really. I've invented a fairy story that I tell her at bedtime. It sort of tells the story of someone who's married but loves someone else at the same time."

"A fairy story? You've got to be kidding me, Harry. What

is it? Beauty and the Beast meets Rumpelstiltskin?"

Harry chuckled. "Not quite," he said. "It's about Inkarta, Rivelo, Estraneo and Lela, and their relationships."

"Bloody hell, Harry. What the hell goes on inside your head, I wonder. What's all that about?"

"It's simple, really," Harry said. "They're all anagrams of real people. Inkarta is Katrina, Rivelo is Oliver and Lela is Ella."

"Then who's this feller Estraneo?"

"I suspected Katrina was having an affair but I didn't know the man's name. He was a stranger, so I called him Estraneo, which is Italian for stranger."

"You're going to have to tell me the story now, Harry. You've got me interested."

Harry wiped his mouth and suggested they walk around the lake while he told her, taking with them a few crumbs and crusts to feed the ducks. An hour later they were sat on their bench.

"That's some story, Harry. It's a bit different to the actual facts and it's got a lot of imagery I don't understand."

"That's the nature of fairy stories," Harry said. "It makes the impossible possible. It's fantasy with moral and social undertones."

"Seems unnecessarily complicated to me," Hazel said with conviction, "but I suppose if Ella's used to fairy stories then she'll probably accept it as normal. But how're you going to bring it all together?"

Harry shook his head and shrugged. "I don't know yet," he admitted. "I'll think of something."

"Let me see if I've got this right. Oliver is always at work and puts that as his highest priority because he's ambitious. He's taking Katrina for granted and assumed that she'd always be there."

Harry nodded.

"Ella is just being a fifteen year old girl. Her priority is her hair, school and boys. She's part of a loving family that provides for her growing up and pays for all her needs."

"Well, that's putting it a bit bluntly, but I suppose so," said Harry.

"Katrina is a different kettle of fish," Hazel continued sagely. "She's at that difficult age isn't she? She's not much younger than me. She's discovered there's more to life than washing and ironing and running a house. She's woken up to the fact that she can do what the hell she likes – within reason. And more than that, she's found out that there's more than one compatible guy out there. Instead of just shagging someone …"

Harry grimaced.

"… she's started an affair. Her biggest problem, I think, is she's fallen in love. If that's the case, she's got some difficult decisions to make. What do you think?"

"I think you've probably hit the nail on the head. Katrina's all over the place at the minute. She's leaving Ella to me, and that's not right. But I understand why she's doing it. She has to sort it out quickly. She has to decide what she's going to do. I'll support whatever decision she makes. I might not like it but I'll go along with it." He paused for a moment then said, "It just goes to show how the actions of one person can affect the lives and futures of so many people."

Hazel bowed her head. "Don't I know it."

Harry regretted his last remark. He wasn't thinking about Hazel's situation at all. He'd been concerned about Katrina and was verbalising his thought processes. He silently berated himself for his insensitivity.

"There is a school of thought that if you do nothing at all, things will work themselves out anyway," he said as a compromise. "C'mon, Hazel, let's get you home."

They walked past the lake and out through the main gate. Soon they were back at Hazel's house, where she dismissed Harry's offer to stay with her a while longer.

"Thanks, Harry," she said, "but you've got other problems to sort out. I need some time to think."

Harry went home deflated and frustrated at the same time.

"Life's a bitch at times," he muttered to himself as he flopped into his favourite chair.

He resolved to contact Hazel every day to make sure she was ok. He didn't know if that would be welcomed or not, but he was concerned enough to risk it. He enjoyed having an excuse to talk to her. He guiltily admitted to himself that she brightened his day, and he knew that she liked his company. He liked her natural smile, how she made him feel important when he visited her or bumped into her strolling through the park. There was always a silver lining to life.

Soon, though, he was napping. It was the middle of a long day.

9

Two weeks passed in which the shilly-shallying surrounding Katrina and Oliver's separation lumbered on. Ella was aloof from all of it, either by effect or by design. Harry felt that he was in no man's land, acting as some sort of umpire or arbitration service. All he wanted to do was live his own life, under his own terms and conditions, and when he told Katrina this, she had stood face to face with him and said, "Yes, Dad, and so do I." Harry had decided not to mention Ella's life at that time for fear of fanning some emotional flames.

Nevertheless, things would have to be said soon. Procrastination was an enemy all on its own.

Harry had spoken to Oliver on two occasions, once at his office and once after work, in a pub. The first meeting consisted of Oliver asking one question – a polite enquiry about Ella and how she was coping – followed by a diatribe pointing out that the separation was all Katrina's fault. The rest of the time consisted of Oliver showing him how successful a businessman he was. The underlying message was that Katrina must be crazy to abandon her lifestyle – ruining him in the process – for some fling with another man. Harry endured the pretence and tried to suggest a reasoned response, but he gave up half way through. He didn't have the heart for it and Oliver wasn't listening in any case. He was a good man, and Harry liked him, but he was a little bit predictable, and limited, in his view of the world. He was egocentric, ambitious and blinkered.

The second meeting was a little more sociable. After brief, cordial exchanges that established that little had changed since their first meeting, Oliver consumed the best part of a bottle of Italian red wine with some scampi and chips. His pretence of living a glamorous lifestyle and having a cultured existence was shattered by that one meal. Over the course of the evening, he became louder and more gregarious until Harry managed to chivvy him into leaving.

Harry felt sorry for him. Without apportioning blame, he saw that Oliver's world was crumbling, but Oliver didn't have the capacity to notice, or, if he did, didn't have the motivation to do anything about it.

Harry saw Katrina every day. Mostly because she visited Ella, but there had been a few times when she'd called early to have minor discussions about Ella that would have been impossible had she been there. It was during one of these discussions that he'd mentioned Will.

It was a Thursday afternoon just before Ella was due back from school.

"What do you want to know about him, Dad?"

"Whatever you want to tell me," he replied guardedly. "I don't want to pry into your affairs." He pulled a face at the unintended pun, which Katrina failed to notice. "I know next to nothing about a man who might be responsible for the welfare of my granddaughter sometime in the future."

It was a good question, which Katrina acknowledged with a smile. She realised her father had borne the brunt of Ella's upbringing in the recent past. He was more than capable of looking after her, but it was an imposition on him that needed qualifying.

Katrina assembled the information from all corners of her brain and explained her position slowly and deliberately. She reiterated how she had met Will and how they had fallen in love.

"The situation at the moment is that Will has asked me to marry him," she said.

Harry's brow furrowed. "I thought …"

Katrina raised her hand to silence him.

"He's already married," she continued. "He's asked his wife for a divorce, but she's a Catholic and isn't too keen on upsetting the family applecart. They've lived separate lives under the same roof for several years, mainly because of the kids, who've now left home, been to University and are living away. Will's wife, Maria, has a mother who is still alive and is a devout Catholic. Maria won't contemplate a divorce until her mother is dead. The mother is nearly eighty and in poor health. Will is ten years older than me." She stopped. "Do you need any more information?" she asked, almost daring him to do so.

"You've obviously made a decision to go with Will," Harry said. "When were you going to tell me? Or Oliver? Or Ella?"

Katrina admitted her mistake immediately. "I'm sorry, Dad. I think I decided last week some time, but I was trying to get myself used to the idea before telling anyone else. Will and I will be spending a lot more time in each other's company, although it's impossible to actually live together, what with the commitments we both have in our former lives."

"You talk as though your new life has started already. What about Ella?"

The first shadows of doubt crossed Katrina's face. "I was hoping she could stay here for the moment, Dad. Is that alright?"

Harry heaved himself out of the chair and paced the

lounge carpet. "I love having her here. You know that. But her proper place is with you. Now you know I wouldn't advocate her staying under the same roof as you and … er … Will, at the moment, but the sooner she's told about the situation the sooner she can get used to it, or react to it, for that matter."

"I know, Dad. It's … difficult."

"Oh, it's difficult alright. The trouble is, the longer you leave it the worse it'll be. You'll have to seize the bull by the horns, love. Believe me it's the only option."

Just then Harry received a text message from Hazel. It said: *He's gone.*

Harry froze. A message out of the blue, simple, potent, life changing. A cold hand squeezed his heart. He said to Katrina, "I've got to go. A friend needs me."

Katrina looked puzzled, her confusion apparent. "But what about Ella? She's due in from school?"

Harry's response was direct and forceful. "You're here aren't you? Be a mother." He hurriedly put on his jacket. "I'm sorry, Katrina, my friend's needs are greater than yours at the moment. I'll be back later."

Within ten minutes he had parked in Hazel's drive and was knocking on the door.

Hazel answered the door, smiled and said, "Thanks, Harry. I thought you'd come. Hope I'm not being a nuisance."

Harry noted that Hazel seemed too composed, too coiffured. She wore a light layer of make-up, her hair was too neatly brushed and she wore a new emerald green dress. He recognised the signs of over-reaction in someone who had just lost a loved one.

He walked into the lounge and stood next to the fireplace like some Victorian gentleman waiting to hear an explanation of a heinous crime. He couldn't think of what to say. What do you say in these situations? He raised his eyebrows and waited for Hazel to say something to him.

She walked up to him and put her arms around his chest in a bear hug. She squeezed him with surprising strength. Her breathing was hard and deliberate as she tried to contain the rising emotion.

They remained like that until her grip slackened and Harry was able to gently hold her away to arm's length so he could see her face.

She said, "He didn't wake up today. They took his breakfast and he was gone. He was all alone when he died, Harry. Isn't that a shame, to end your life without anyone being there to close your eyes or say a prayer, or just say goodbye? That's awful."

Harry closed his eyes and sighed deeply. He knew what she meant. Thelma had died alone, even though there were people in the house at the time. "You can't choose a time to die," he said. "It's always inconvenient." He didn't want to roll out the platitudes that well-intentioned people normally said at these times, so he said nothing more.

They sat down and held hands. "What happens now?" Harry asked after a while.

"The people at Sunnybrooks are handling everything. They asked me if I wanted to do it, but I said no." Hazel paused briefly before adding, "It's a strange feeling, Harry. I feel relieved in some way. It's as if a huge weight's been lifted from my shoulders. I don't feel responsible any more. I know I sound callous, but I'm glad he's dead. I know I should be crying like a baby, but I'm not. I'm frightening myself, Harry. Why aren't I reacting normally?"

Harry thought for a moment and then said, "What's normal? I've met a few people who've been grieving over the death of a loved one and none of them reacted in the same way. When Thelma died I went out and bought a paper. I went to the park to read it as if nothing had happened. I came back home – Katrina was past herself – and asked for a bacon sandwich. The top and bottom of it is that you don't know how to react because it's never happened to you before."

The telephone rang and Hazel rose to answer it. She had a brief one-sided conversation with a deep male voice before she replaced the phone in its cradle.

"That was Doctor Bradley from Sunnybrooks. They want me to go in and complete some formalities."

"I'll take you," volunteered Harry.

"No thanks, Harry. That's sweet of you, but, as you see, I'm ok. I want to see him for the last time anyway."

She kissed him on the cheek and squeezed his hand in appreciation.

"Ring me. Any time," said Harry.

Hazel knew he meant it. It gave her an enormous amount of satisfaction to know that if she did fall apart at some stage there'd be someone there who could put the pieces back together again.

"I will," she said.

Harry drove home and arrived in time for dinner – a pasta bake. A harassed looking Katrina had made the meal, which was being picked over by Ella who looked as if she'd been crying. He sighed resignedly, exchanged looks with Katrina, who shook her head to indicate she didn't know what was going on and, what's more, seemed afraid to find out, so he just shrugged and gave an exasperated shake of his head and munched his way through two helpings of pasta. He thought about Hazel's problems and compared them to those being presented around the dinner table. There was no comparison.

He glanced at his daughter's and his granddaughter's plates. Both still held scattered heaps of food. He shrugged again. One of his mottos was to eat food while you can because you never know when you'll eat again. He sat a few moments, then picked up the plates, scraped off the food and started washing the dishes.

Ella continued to sit and mope. She was hungry but hadn't felt like eating. Her mother was floating around trying hard not to upset her and obviously wanted to be somewhere else – anywhere else; she was constantly looking at her watch and checking her mobile phone, which must have been on 'vibrate only' as Ella had not heard it make incoming message sounds.

She wanted to say something but was too concerned with internal questions to be bothered. Why is the adult world so complicated? Why can't everyone be happy?

She got sick of seeing the sad faces in the room, excused herself and went to her room. She noticed the questioning glances between her grandad and her mother as they tried to work out what was going on with her, but she wasn't going to help them out until she saw her father tomorrow.

Half an hour later Katrina shouted upstairs that she was leaving.

Ella shouted, "'Bye" and left it at that. Her mother would know that something was troubling her and she'd probably ask her grandad to find out what it was.

An hour or so passed before Harry knocked on the door. Ella was sitting cross legged on her bed reading a magazine. Harry looked at Ella's school books piled on the desk.

Ella said, "Before you start, I've done my homework and revision."

"Nothing to do with me, Tuppence. None of my business. You know what's best for you. It's worked well so far."

Ella knitted her brow then asked, "Has my mum asked you to find out what the matter is?"

"She's concerned, love, so am I, but we figure that if you've got something to say you'll say it in your own time."

"Thanks, Grandad. I need to see Dad before I say anything. I need to ask him a question."

"Anything I can help you with?" Harry enquired.

"No, not yet," Ella replied.

"Do you want me to tell you a story?"

"No thanks, Grandad," Ella said sternly "I'm not in the mood to listen to any more tales, or should I say lies."

Harry raised his eyes and grimaced. What was going on inside her mind he wondered. "What do you mean?"

"Oh, nothing, Grandad. I'm sorry. I've got a lot on my mind that needs sorting out. I'll tell you as soon as I can".

"Ok, Tuppence. I'm here if you want me. Nite nite."

"Nite, Grandad," then added, "Love you."

Harry beamed back at her. "And I love you too," he said.

Harry closed the bedroom door behind him. She's annoyed about something, he thought, but it wasn't anything to do with him. That's what the 'love you' was for, to absolve him of any culpability in the matter. Even so, it would appear that her father knew all the answers. "That'll be a first," he murmured as he walked down the stairs to do his security check before going to bed. He would be pleased to get to bed and end this day. Perhaps tomorrow would bring him some news that would put a smile on his face, but then again, perhaps not. He was desperate for some good news.

10

There wasn't any good news in the post the next day. Harry was relieved to find that Ella seemed to be less preoccupied than last night, and when Katrina arrived to take her to school she kissed him goodbye and engaged her mother in polite school talk conversation.

Katrina seemed vibrant and talkative. She had left to meet Will last night. Harry presumed they had managed to engineer a night together.

Katrina dropped Ella off at the school gates and they waived to each other as Katrina drove away towards town.

Ella entered a door at the rear of the school and made her way to the front door. She hadn't told her mother or grandfather that she'd been given a free morning to revise for an upcoming exam. She left the school and walked the half mile or so to her father's office. It wasn't quite 8.30am but she knew her father would've been at his desk for at least an hour. Her father had brought her here several times in the past so she knew her way to his office.

She slipped by the Reception Desk without being seen. Mrs Robson was answering a phone, her back turned towards the sliding glass panels in Reception, and making a cup of tea, the limit of her multi-tasking. Ella walked down the short corridor, then turned right. Her father's office was first on the right.

Oliver was engrossed in a file of papers as his daughter walked in. He looked up at her then back down at the file before he realised it was Ella standing in his office and not his secretary.

"Hello, love," he said with a perplexed look on his face. How did you get in here? Why aren't you at school? Is there something wrong?"

All the questions sprang out in a brief moment of confusion.

Ella ignored his questions and approached his desk and sat on a chair she dragged from a table at the side of the room. She adjusted it to face her father, folding her arms and crossing her legs in the process.

"Dad, who's the blonde woman you were with yesterday?"

Oliver's eyes shot up. He immediately replayed the events of yesterday in his memory and wondered how he was going to deflect Ella's questions.

"Who was the woman you were with yesterday. My friend Hannah saw you with a blonde woman, in town, yesterday. I want to know who she was."

Ella thought she was being very cool and detached.

"What?" Oliver said, more than a little flustered. "I don't see what this has got to do with you," he spluttered. Then offered "She's a …" He was going to say client but changed his mind at the last second. "… colleague. We went out for lunch. Her name's Fiona." He smiled nervously. Momentarily, an image of his 'colleague' half naked and lying on her bed flashed through his mind, an event he hoped would be repeated very soon.

"Do you always hold hands with your colleagues, and stroke the backs of their necks?" Ella asked facetiously.

Oliver felt a big, cold void growing inside him. "What?" he said again to give himself breathing space. "Hannah? Who's this Hannah? What lies is she telling you?"

"Dad, my friend Hannah was having lunch with her father yesterday in Angelo's Trattoria when she saw you with Fiona." She uttered the name with contempt. "She says you couldn't keep your hands off her and you were embarrassing. Hannah's been to our house and she recognised you."

Oliver had a vague memory of a mature looking girl with a man in his fifties sitting at a table nearby. She had seemed familiar somehow, but he thought the middle-aged man accompanying her was just another guy like himself who was trying to get some pleasure out of life by entertaining his secretary or something. He groaned inwardly. He'd never cheated on Katrina in his life. It was just his luck that he'd been spotted with another woman while he and Katrina were temporarily apart. He recalled that he'd been a bit familiar with Fiona but not to the extent of being embarrassing.

"Ok, ok, ok," he stammered. "Fiona is a colleague, she works along the corridor. We were having lunch together, and we were being … friendly, I think it would be fair to say."

"Are you having sex with her?" Ella asked bluntly.

"Ella!" Once more wrong footed by his daughter. "What are you saying?"

"It's a simple question, Dad. Are you having sex with Fiona?"

"No, I'm not. And I can't see what business it is of yours anyway," Oliver said sanctimoniously in an effort to gain the high moral ground.

"Dad, I don't have to spell it out to you do I? You and Mum are separated. That doesn't mean it's finished. If you start having sex with other people we'll never get back together again. Why don't you tell Fiona you won't see her again and then you can behave yourself?"

Oliver was flattened. He was being chastised by his own daughter for having a relationship that hadn't taken off yet, while his wife, her mother, was having an affair with another man. It was too much for him. He felt his anger building. He got up and marched to the office door and slammed it shut, then whirled around to face his daughter. He leaned over her as she sat in the visitor's chair.

"Now you listen to me, young lady," he hissed with barely controlled anger. "You have no right to talk to me like that. I'm your father. I'm not the one who's breaking this family up; your mother is. I'm the one who's worked all the hours God sends us so that we can have a very good standard of living." He punctuated each sentence with a raised forefinger.

"I haven't gone out of my way to conceal a friendship with someone else. Alright, yes, I was trying to convince another woman that spending a little bit of time with me would be beneficial to us both. Yes, that means trying to have sex with her. But I'm only doing what your mother's been doing for months."

As soon as he said the words he regretted it.

A look of astonishment, then shock, spread over Ella's face. Her eyes never left him. They were searching for a hint of disbelief, but there was none.

Oliver stood up and went to the office door. He opened it and saw his secretary coming out of her office. "Can you get me two coffees please. White, no sugar, soon as you like."

Oliver sat down on the edge of his desk. He knew he had wrecked his daughter's dreams of returning to a happy family life. He could see she was crushed. There was a battle going on inside his head – one side justifying his actions, the other admonishing him for his anger and selfishness. Still, everything he said was true. Why should he feel guilty for telling it like it was? He would be the first to admit that diplomacy wasn't his strong point. He shouldn't have told her. And he knew Katrina would be absolutely livid.

The secretary knocked on the door and entered with a tray holding two mugs of steaming hot coffee, twists of sugar and a small glass jug of milk. Her fixed smile disappeared as soon as she gauged the frosty atmosphere pervading the office. She placed the tray on the desk and swiftly backed out.

Oliver picked up one mug and put milk in it before handing it to Ella. His voice softened. "Here you are, love," he said. Then after some moments of reflection added, "I'm sorry you had to find out this way. I never should've said what I did, although every word of it is true."

He tried to hold Ella's hand but she pulled away.

Ella slumped in the chair like a discarded teddy bear. Her stone-faced composure was evaporating by the second. Emotionally, she was quickly regressing through the years to become a confused little girl again. Tears were forming at the corner of her eyes. She tried to hold them back, but failed. Soon she was issuing quiet little sobs – but saying nothing.

Oliver glanced at his desk. There were things to do and he could do without a pantomime in his office. He gave a fleeting look through the frosted glass window wondering if his secretary was informing the world that 'something was going on in the Boss's office.' Only a few people knew of his separation from Katrina, but a bit of tittle-tattle and an emotionally unstable daughter in the office would allow people to jump to their own conclusions.

He walked to the main office window and looked out into the car park. A Nissan 4 x 4 steered towards a reserved parking bay. It came to a halt and the curvaceous Fiona stepped out. A faint stirring in Oliver's loins reminded him of how close he had been to an afternoon of passionate 'meetings' yesterday.

"Is that her?" Ella's said, moving silently to his side.

In the car park, Fiona saw Oliver at the window. She gave a little wave and knowing smile that betrayed their intimacy.

"She looks nice," Ella said, trying to be non-judgemental.

"She's a very nice person."

"Nicer than Mum?"

Oliver turned to her and said, "Don't, Ella. Let's not go there. Your mother's changed. She's not the same person I married."

"And you're the same man, are you? Even I know that people change, Dad. But why does it have to affect me?"

Oliver tried to hug his daughter, but she evaded his outstretched arms and scurried to the door.

"I'm going, Dad."

Oliver protested, but Ella dismissed it with a shake of the head. "I'm ok. Honest I am. It's been a bit of a shock, but I'm ok." Her eyes were dry but red rimmed.

She's like her mother, Oliver thought. She can switch it on and off like a tap – like most women. "I'll speak to your mother and tell her what's happened," he said, dreading the prospect. "Are sure you're alright?"

"Yes, Dad, I'm fine. I'll call you later," Ella said, although she had no intention of doing so.

She left the office and passed through the Reception just as Fiona was signing in. A pungent, floral perfume overwhelmed Ella as she passed by her. She groaned and covered her mouth theatrically while pretending to gag. She rushed out the door to leave a bewildered Fiona and the receptionist gaping after her.

She ran down the street towards her grandfather's house. She'd ask him what to do. He'd be really upset when she told him that her mother was having an affair. She raced through the park just in case he was feeding the ducks. She reached his favourite bench, but he wasn't there, it was occupied by a surprised woman about the same age as her mother. The woman looked as though she'd been crying as well, although when she smiled to acknowledge Ella's presence, her face lit up. Ella returned the smile and said, "I'm sorry for startling you. I was expecting to see my grandad here. He comes most days to feed the ducks."

Before the woman had time to reply, Ella ran off again. The woman sighed and said to herself, "I think there's some trouble brewing, Harry."

Ella reached her grandfather's house and found it empty. Where was he, she thought. She sat down and waited, hoping he would come back soon. It gave her some time to think.

Her mother was having an affair with another man. Her father was trying to have sex with another woman. And this was supposed to be a trial separation. There was no way that her parents would be reconciled if that was the situation. Then why don't they just leave each other and get on with life?

The situation seemed straight forward until she thought about her own predicament. Where would she go? Who would look after her?

She tried to rationalise things. They'll ask me who I want to stay with, won't they? I love Mum, but she's having sex with someone who I haven't even met. Dad's always at work, and I don't want to live in a place where he brings 'colleagues' back. I'll stay with Grandad. He'll have me. He's always there for me when I need him. She looked around the room. Grandad isn't here now, and I need him, she thought.

The reality of an uncertain future caused her to catch her breath. She felt anxiety rising in her chest. Suddenly, she felt alone. She couldn't wait for her grandad any longer. She had to speak to her mother. Surely all this was just a misunderstanding;

if her mother was having an affair she would've noticed. Every programme she had seen on television said that it was obvious when someone was seeing someone else. All the magazines she'd read told about secret meetings, changes in behaviour and wearing clothes that were smarter or more modern than usual. That hadn't happened to her mother. She was always smart, especially since she'd been working as a volunteer at that charity shop.

Oh, she thought unconsciously.

There hadn't been any nights out without her dad. In fact the only time her mother hadn't been around was when she went to that charity conference a couple of months back. She must've been so busy because she came back exhausted and looking very tired.

Oh, she thought again.

She recalled that her father had asked why she was taking her best cocktail dress to a charity function. Mum had said there would be a lot of bigwigs there that needed to be cultivated. She hadn't quite known what that meant.

All of a sudden it dawned on her that what she was describing was exactly what the magazines had said bore the hallmarks of an affair. There were no secret meetings because the meetings were at the charity shop. The changes in appearance were camouflaged by the necessity to be presentable at work. Her behaviour and conversation had centred on work.

She desperately tried to recall snatches of conversation between her mother and her father regarding her mother's work. None of it seemed to be relevant. But the key seemed to be the charity shop.

Ella looked at her watch. Her mother would be at the shop now. She decided to go to there and tell her mother what had happened that morning and confront her about what her dad had said.

11

Harry ambled through the park carrying a stale French stick he'd managed to cadge from his friend at the bakery. It was an occasional treat for the ducks, although they probably couldn't tell the difference. Nevertheless, Harry thought he was doing them a favour – variety is the spice of life, he mused.

It was a nice, bright day with hardly a cloud in the sky, and he was humming an old 60s ballad to himself while his mind's eye was watching his debonair, twenty year old image dancing slowly with a tall, leggy redhead around a film set style ballroom. He rounded the bushes that acted as a wind break to his favourite park bench and saw Hazel sitting there staring contemplatively out across the lake. He saw at once that she'd been crying. Her distress brought him back down to earth.

"Hello, love," he said as he sat next to her.

"Hi, Harry," Hazel replied. "I think you've just missed your granddaughter. There was a young girl here not so long ago looking for her grandad. She looked a bit agitated."

Harry's spirits dropped. Ella should have been at school, although she'd recently mentioned that there were free periods coming up that were supposed to be study time. He hadn't realised one of them was today. She hadn't said anything.

"Agitated?" he asked.

"Yes, she seemed in a rush to find you and ran off towards your house. I presumed she'd meet you on your way here."

"I left earlier to go to the High Street to get this." He pointed to the French stick.

He checked his mobile phone and saw that there were no missed calls or messages. He rang Ella's mobile, but it didn't connect.

"Couldn't have been that important if she didn't leave a message," he said almost abstractedly. "Never mind that. How're you?"

"So so," Hazel said. "It's Fino's funeral tomorrow."

The statement introduced a respectful silence.

"I'm just having a private service because there's no-one to invite. Life goes on as normal, doesn't it?"

Harry nodded sympathetically and considered volunteering to attend the funeral to support her, but decided against it. It would be an unnecessary complication.

"Do you want to meet tomorrow afternoon and have a meal or do something? Anything at all?" he asked.

She reached across to hold his hand.

"Thanks for the offer, Harry, but I've got a hospital appointment tomorrow afternoon." She pointed to her lap. "I've been having a bit of trouble down below. You know: women's troubles."

Harry knew that women's troubles were many and varied and beyond his realm of understanding. He didn't enquire any further. He turned his attention to the ducks, which were paddling on the water pretending not to notice them, until he stood up. He broke the French stick in half and handed one end to Hazel, who accepted it with a smile. They both stood at the edge of the lake and spent the next five minutes bringing joy to its greedy residents.

***

107

Will was already at the shop when Katrina had arrived that morning. There were two customers browsing through some books and CDs. They had both smiled at Katrina, commenting on the weather. Katrina had said hello to them and had greeted Will similarly. Front of shop Katrina and Will were focused and professional, but behind the scenes they were constantly kissing and caressing. Their professionalism had stopped them from making love there, but on more than one occasion their passions had resulted in frenzied sex in a hotel room ten miles away. That morning, they'd managed their first grope within ten minutes of Katrina arriving, only seconds after the two customers had left.

Will had popped out to do some business at the bank.

Katrina busied herself reorganising a rack of clothing that had been ravaged by a couple of grannies looking for a bargain. One of them had complained that things were too expensive. Where else can you get a pure wool skirt for £5? Katrina thought. The other woman had asked her if she had a blue dress in a different size. They obviously didn't appreciate the finer points of a charity shop – everything on display had been donated by people who no longer wanted them, for whatever reason.

Her thoughts turned, inevitably, to Will.

He was a good person to work with. He had a business type of brain that was organised and well prepared. He'd often spoken of his desire to run his own small business, but he didn't have the financial backing or familial support. He'd been frank with Katrina from day one. He was married to a woman who refused him a divorce based on her family's religious views, yet she'd developed a relationship with another man years ago. She spent most weekends with him. Most of the family knew the situation and turned a blind eye towards it. Their children, now adults, had grown up within this semi-detached relationship, but it hadn't damaged them in any apparent way. Both parents had made a supreme effort to normalise life. They were still friends, but not lovers. They lived in the same house and shared responsibilities, but they lived separate lives.

The front door opened, ringing the old fashioned bell above it. Katrina looked to welcome the new customer and was surprised to see Ella. She was even more surprised when Ella closed the door behind her and turned the CLOSED sign towards the street.

"Ella! What on earth are you doing?" she said, moving towards the door.

Ella stood in front of it and spoke softly and slowly. "I need to speak to you privately," she said before taking a deep breath and shouting, "Now!"

Dread surged through Katrina. Something had happened and she automatically knew she wasn't going to like it.

"What's the matter?" she asked, before trying to reassert the parent–child equilibrium by demanding, "And who do you think you're talking to?"

Ella pointed at her mother. "I'm talking to you, Mother!" she said derisorily. "Or should I say a slut who pretends to be my mother!"

Katrina flushed. Ella had never spoken to her like this before. "What are you talking about, Ella? What's going on?"

"You're shagging someone. That's why you broke up our family. That's why I'm living with Grandad and that's why Dad's turning into a sex mad letch. It's your fault. You've ruined our lives just because you want to have sex with other people. You're a selfish whore ..."

Katrina instinctively slapped Ella hard across the face.

Ella burst into tears and tried to reopen the door to escape.

Katrina was glad that the old door lock was a contrary

one that needed a little bit of know-how to open it properly.

Ella wailed in frustration then ran into the back of the shop sobbing.

Katrina stood motionless trying to control her breathing and rising anxiety. "Oh, my God," she whispered to herself. It had happened. Ella knew. How had she found out? Guilt swamped her. What was she going to do? It was all such a mess.

A customer tried the closed door and then rapped on it.

"Can't you read?" Katrina shouted. "We're closed."

She took a deep breath and wearily sought Ella at the back of the shop, ignoring the continued knocking of the customer on the locked door.

Ella was bowed forward, crying softly, cradling her head in her hands, her elbows resting on her knees. An abstract screensaver slowly bounced around a computer screen. Several boxes of as yet uncatalogued clothing, books and bric-a-brac filled the space between the desk and two chairs, one of which was where Ella sat.

Katrina sat in the other chair and spoke in a quiet, caring, motherly tone. "Come on, dear. Tell me what's happened."

Ella shook her head without looking up. "It's all your fault," she said. "You're having an affair."

Katrina sighed. "I need to know what's going on." Her father had always said that if you've been discovered doing something wrong – don't compound the error by denying it, it'll only make things worse. Admit your guilt and take the consequences. There was a caveat to that. Only admit to what has been discovered, nothing else.

"You know what's going on because you're the one doing it," Ella sobbed.

Katrina maintained her softly, softly approach. "You are making allegations against me, but I don't know what they are.

Tell me what you've been told and we'll discuss it."

She ignored a series of loud knocks on the front door of the shop.

Ella reached for a clean tissue and threw the old one into the waste paper basket. She lifted her head and looked her mother in the face. "How could you, Mum. Why did you do it?"

Katrina's guilt turned to tears that welled in her eyes.

The banging on the front door stopped.

"Ella, please tell me what you've heard," Katrina implored.

"I went to see Dad, because a friend saw him slavering on with a blonde woman in a restaurant. He admitted it, but he said he was only doing what you've been doing for months." Ella searched her mother's face for signs of denial, but found none.

Katrina's shoulders slumped. So that's it. Oliver. He couldn't keep a lid on it. The bastard! She wanted to ring him immediately and give him a mouthful of abuse. Why hadn't he waited? But then again, why wait?

The separation had, in truth, been the first step in the divorce process, although Oliver hadn't been aware of that. What had happened so far was a time-buying exercise to get Katrina, and Ella, accustomed to the broken family syndrome, and then they could take it from there. The current situation was something Katrina hadn't figured on until a bit further down the track, but now that it was here it had to be dealt with before they could move on.

Katrina reached across to tenderly wipe away a tear from the corner of Ella's left eye.

It was a gesture that softened Ella's fears.

"Oh, Mum," she cried, "what's happening?"

Katrina wrapped her arms around her daughter.

"My poor darling," she said. "You don't deserve this."

They hugged each other for a few moments before Ella said, "Are you having an affair, Mum?"

Before she could answer, the back door opened and an anxious looking Will bustled into the room.

"What's going on?" he demanded. "The front door's shut and there's a customer standing outside."

"Can you give us a few seconds please, Will?" Katrina said.

Will took a few seconds to assess the situation. The atmosphere was balanced on a knife edge. He left them alone and went into the shop to re-open the front door where he apologised profusely to the locked out customer.

Katrina said to Ella, "I don't think this is the time or place to talk about these things."

"I need to know, Mum. Can we go home now and talk about it. You can leave here. It's only a voluntary job in a shop after all."

Katrina closed her eyes. That attitude was what she expected from Oliver, not her daughter. Perhaps they'd kept Ella protected from the real world for too long. Nevertheless, her job wasn't as important to her as the love of her daughter, and although she knew she was being manipulated, Katrina agreed. "Ok, love. You dry your eyes and go through the back yard to my car and wait there. I'll tell Will that I'm leaving."

She went into the shop and waited until Will had finished serving the customer.

"I've got to go, Will. Ella's very upset. Oliver's told her I'm having an affair."

"The bloody fool," Will said. "That's fine, love. It's ok. You go and sort it out." Almost as an afterthought he said, "Do you want me to come with you? William's in shortly. I can leave him here for an hour or two."

She shrugged off the offer. "It's too much too soon for her, Will." Let her get used to the idea first, then we'll get together."

She returned to the back room to find Ella gone. Will followed behind.

"Take care love," Will said. He put his arms around her and drew her into a tender embrace. "I love you."

They kissed.

Just then a stone smashed through the window next to the desk scattering shards of glass everywhere. Beyond the window stood Ella, her face distorted with rage.

"It's him!" she shouted. "I should've known. He's the one who you've been shagging all along." She turned and ran out of the yard, passing the car, and into the back lane.

Katrina pushed Will away and ran into the lane to find her. She was gone.

Will brushed away some glass from the desk and the seat that had been occupied by Ella a few moments ago. He sat down wearily. This was yet another drama in a litany of disasters in his relationship with Katrina.

Katrina returned to the shop a few seconds later on the verge of hyperventilation. Her sobs were shallow and rapid and she wheezed like a set of broken bellows.

Will spent ten minutes calming her down until she was able to speak coherently again.

"I have to find her," she said repeatedly.

"She'll be alright," said Will in an effort to reassure her. "She'll make her way back to your dad's place. Maybe you'd better call him and let him know what's happened."

"No, not yet. I have to speak to Ella. I'll go to Dad's now and see if she's gone there. If she's not, I'll call him and put him in the picture."

She gathered her things together and started to leave. Will

took hold of her arm.

"Don't," she said, glaring at him. "Haven't you caused enough trouble today?"

I've been here before, he thought. Whenever there'd been problems in the past, her anger and vitriol were poured over him. She'd scorned him many times. He'd counted thirteen occasions when she'd ended their relationship before wanting him back. She'd even asked him to stop being her lover and just be her friend. He was so much in love with her he was prepared to accept any conditions just so he could still see her – even though he knew it would tear him apart. In truth, what she wanted was a nuclear family and a storybook style marriage with the excitement of an extramarital affair that could be accessed whenever she needed it. And, any negative aspects of the relationship lay fairly and squarely at his door. After all, wasn't he a male predator of unsuspecting and vulnerable women?

Katrina left the shop and climbed into her car. She caught a glimpse of herself in the rear view mirror and saw a face that reflected this morning's trauma. She applied a layer of lipstick in an attempt to repair some of the damage and restore a bit of confidence. Once she felt calm and collected enough, she drove off.

Will heard the shop bell sound and went to investigate. It doesn't matter what happens in anyone's life, he thought, the world still spins around, night follows day, and people always want to find a bargain in a charity shop.

12

Ella sat in a supermarket café with an untouched milky coffee that was going cold. She tried to think things through for the umpteenth time. The explosive anger that had caused her to throw a stone through the window of the charity shop was gone, replaced by a feeling of desolation and loneliness. She felt abandoned by both parents; they'd found lives beyond the family, but none that included her.

She wished Will would die. Not a nasty death – just die in his sleep or something. That would cure the problem. Her mother would then see sense and go back to her dad and, after an apology or two, everything would return to normal and she could start enjoying herself again. Her mobile vibrated for the sixth or seventh time, but she didn't even look to see who it was.

Trade in the café was brisk. There were pensioners with tea and cakes, suited youngsters with flavoured water and a panini, and young mums who fed their screaming kids with pieces of sausage roll or a packet of crisps while chatting to their friends about how busy they were. Ella gulped her coffee, vacated her booth and deposited the empty cup in the bin. She managed to avoid being knocked over by a man on a disability scooter motoring at ten miles an hour up to the cigarette counter, and walked out into bright sunshine, which she took a moment to get used to. The warmth of the sun and the blueness of the sky contrasted with the darkness of her life at that moment.

***

Katrina had been at her father's house for almost an hour waiting for Ella to come back. She hadn't rung the school in case they'd asked some difficult questions that might embarrass Ella, or herself, at some later date. She thought it unlikely that Ella would go to school anyway, because she was upset. Normally, she'd come here, but Katrina had spoken briefly to her dad on his mobile and she wasn't with him. The only other place she'd go was to her father, who was at work.

Katrina's stomach grumbled. She hadn't eaten anything yet so she made herself a slice of toast and a cup of tea. It took up another fifteen minutes. She looked at her watch. It was lunch time. She needed to speak to Oliver. She quickly rinsed her cup and plate and straightened the cushions. She closed the door and got into her car. Ten minutes later she was driving into the car park. Coincidently, she parked next to Oliver's car. She smiled wryly; this was the first time in a long time they'd been side by side in anything.

***

Harry was worried. First, he'd missed Ella in the park when he went to get the French stick and she hadn't answered her mobile, and, secondly, he'd had a telephone call from Katrina asking if he'd seen Ella in the last hour or so. Katrina had been deliberately light and fluffy in tone but Harry detected traces of anxiety there. She couldn't fool him. He'd been seeing through her lies and half-truths since she'd uttered her first words. Not that there had been many occasions when that had happened, and certainly none that had serious repercussions.

According to Katrina, she only told little white lies, usually to protect people or to stop them from worrying, but Harry knew that some of those lies were lighter shades of grey, and some were darker than that. The lies she must've told Oliver to conduct her affair with Will were bordering on royal blue.

Harry wished he could've heard those conversations between Katrina and Oliver, because whenever Katrina told a lie she had a habit of raising both eyebrows. He could picture those eyebrows rising during their last telephone conversation.

"I have to go," he had said to Hazel who had overheard everything.

"Go where?" Hazel asked.

Harry shrugged. "Home, I suppose. Sooner or later Ella'll come back and she'll need someone."

"Don't try to molly-coddle her, Harry, she needs time to adjust. All her life people have made decisions for her, usually in her favour, and now she's got the weight of the world on her shoulders. It's hard, but she'll get through it soon enough."

Harry looked hard at Hazel. He didn't agree with all she'd said, but the last thing he wanted was an argument on the subject. "I'll be off, then. I'll let you know what happens."

He walking away but remembered Fino's funeral. Once again he'd been so preoccupied with his own family situation that he had neglected the feelings of his friend. He returned to Hazel and kissed her on the cheek. He picked up her left hand and held it. The diamond in her engagement ring was dull, the pattern on the wedding band scuffed and worn.

"I want you to let me know if I can help in any way. I mean that, Hazel. Will you?" he said seriously.

Hazel nodded. "Thanks, Harry. I will. But I think you've got things to worry about other than me. I'll manage. I've managed all these years by myself. I'm used to it."

"Sometimes you just need to hold on to somebody," Harry said squeezing her hand.

"Thanks for being my friend, Harry."

Harry smiled and walked away with a heavy heart. He wanted to show more support than he had done so far, but Hazel was right; he had other things on his mind, none of which were within his control. Ironically, he usually advised others to concentrate only on what they could control. He found himself thinking about how important Hazel was to him; he knew he could rely on her to dispense words of wisdom if he went to her with a problem and he was confident that she'd always be there for him.

Ella wasn't home when he got there, although he noticed a cup and plate had been washed and placed on the draining board. Katrina, he thought.

So, Katrina was actually looking for Ella. That suggested urgency. Something bad had happened. He tried to ring Katrina but the call was deflected to a recorded message. He said, "Katrina, it's your dad. Is something wrong? Ring me when you get this message."

He rang Ella. It rang twice then went off. She didn't want to talk to him yet.

Harry sat down. His family was in turmoil, his friend's husband had died and all he could do was sit in an armchair and worry. He bit his lip and waited. Someone would call, eventually.

***

Katrina made a bee-line for Reception. Her mobile rang. She glanced at it and saw that it was her father. She ignored it. He would leave a message. It rang off and seconds later issued a tone indicating a message had been received. She hauled open the glass doors as she listened to her father. She replaced the phone in her bag as she reached the counter. She would ring him later. Ella obviously wasn't there.

The receptionist smiled her corporate greeting and asked her to sign the visitor's book before directing her to Oliver's office.

"I'll ring and tell him you're here," she said.

Katrina smiled back. By the time she did that she'd be entering his office.

She heard the phone ring as she reached his door. She didn't bother knocking and went straight in to find Oliver replacing the handset in its cradle. A blonde woman was sitting in a seat next to his desk. She was wearing a pink dress that was a little too short for work. Her perfume was pleasant but overpowering – as though it had been applied a few moments ago.

Oliver's expression was one of shock and apprehension. The blonde tugged at the hem of her dress and uncrossed her legs into a more business-like pose.

Oliver was the first to recover composure and made the introductions. "Fiona this is my wife, Katrina. Katrina this is Fiona, a colleague of mine." He then said to Fiona "It's probably a good time to break for lunch. Can we resume about three?"

Fiona picked up a briefcase and said, "Sure. See you at three." She smiled sweetly at Katrina and said "Nice to meet you" as she left.

Katrina noticed Oliver gazing at Fiona's legs.

"Does she bark?" asked Katrina.

"Does she bark? What do you mean?"

"I thought all dogs barked," Katrina said acidly.

"That's beneath even you," Oliver replied.

Katrina sat down in the chair vacated by Fiona. The

remnants of her perfume still lingered. "Smells like a whorehouse," she said.

"That's rich coming from you," Oliver shot back.

They both glared at each other assessing their relative positions.

Katrina finally said, "You had no right to tell Ella about Will and me. That was cruel, Oliver. She didn't deserve to find out that way."

Oliver held up his hand in acknowledgement of wrong-doing and said, "I'm sorry it happened the way it did, Katrina. Honest I am. I regret that very much. She caught me on the hop and started making allegations about Fiona and me. It just came out …" His voice trailed off.

Katrina saw that Oliver was genuinely upset about how things had been revealed to their daughter. She felt a modicum of sympathy for him. He'd put up with a situation for months that she certainly wouldn't have been able to cope with. The realisation calmed her. "Ok, so what are we going to do now that it's out in the open?"

"How the hell do I know?" Oliver said. "This isn't my fault."

Katrina groaned. "For Christ's sake, Oliver, forget about me being a scarlet woman and you being the white knight. We're talking about our daughter and her future. Whatever happens between us comes second to Ella's welfare."

Oliver sighed and nodded. "I'm sorry, you're right. Ella is our main concern." He looked at Katrina and said, "I suppose we are finished then?"

Katrina was surprised to see a look of hope on Oliver's face.

She said, "It's over between us, Oliver. It has been for some time. We just didn't see things getting away from us. I know it was me who committed adultery …"

Oliver stiffened and assumed a pious pose. At last, he thought, confirmation of her indiscretion.

"… but circumstances inside our marriage allowed it to happen."

Oliver started to protest, but Katrina ignored him and continued.

"… let's not get bogged down in the whys and wherefores of what went wrong between us. Let's have a civilised conversation about what happens next."

It was an appeal that Oliver reluctantly accepted.

"Ok," he said. "Where do we start?"

For the next fifteen minutes they talked about the morning's sequence of events, until they both had an understanding of what had happened. Oliver was dismayed that his daughter was missing. They discussed their options and decided that Ella was a sensible child who would revert back to being the loving home-bird they had brought her up to be. She would go home after an hour or two. She would certainly want to talk to her grandad.

***

Harry was dozing in his chair when Katrina rang him.

"Hello?"

"Dad, it's me. Is Ella there?"

"No, she's not. What's going on?"

Katrina sighed. She didn't want to get involved in a difficult discussion over the phone. "She's found out about Will and me."

"Found out? Who told her?

"Oliver. Accidentally."

Back in the office, Oliver looked suitably remorseful.

Harry frowned. How the hell do you tell something

accidentally?

Katrina continued, "I'll tell you the whole story when I get back. But we don't know where Ella is. Have you any ideas."

Harry knew his granddaughter. "She'll come here when she's calmed down." He told Katrina that Ella had already been to the park to try and find him today. "It's was only a matter of time before she comes here. I'll let you know when she arrives."

"Ok, Dad."

"Oh, Katrina …"

"Yes?"

"… tell Oliver he's a bloody idiot."

"Ok, Dad."

She didn't. She replaced the phone and said, "I'll speak to you again shortly. Are we clear that we're going to treat each other as sensible adults and not go down the path of all-out war, for the sake of Ella?"

Oliver said, "I don't know why I'm being reasonable here, but ok. Katrina … no dirty tricks, eh?"

"I have no intention of pulling any tricks as long as you recognise the fact that Will and I will be a lot more open about our relationship now. And you can pursue Dogface to your heart's content." She faked a kiss with a long mmmwwwaaaaaah, then said, "Seriously, Oliver, let's not make things more difficult than they actually are."

She left the room and exited the building without signing out, much to Mrs Robson's disgust.

13

Harry put the phone down and looked at the clock. Ella had been missing for nearly two hours. She wouldn't go to school. She'd probably go to the shopping centre and have a walk around, or have a coffee or something. He was confident that she wouldn't come to any harm and she'd be back shortly.

She arrived just as Harry had made himself a sandwich and poured a mug of tea.

He said, "Just like your mother. She knows when the kettle's boiled."

Ella huffed and puffed and slouched into an armchair.

"I hope I'm not like her," she said derisorily. "She's a slut!"

Harry exhaled theatrically and plonked his plate and mug heavily on the table. He looked at her sternly and said, "Whatever your mother has done, or is doing, does not make her a slut. You obviously know nothing at all about what's really happening and all you are doing is demonstrating how little you know of the real world and how it works." He grabbed his sandwich and took a large bite out of it. He chewed and chewed, giving him time to control his anger.

Ella sat and sulked, twisting a lock of hair then releasing it when it got too tight.

Harry took another bite of his sandwich and slurped his tea. His jaw was bouncing up and down rapidly like a ravenous rabbit. He felt the tension easing, but the tightness across his chest remained. He finished the sandwich and set down the mug. He cleared his throat and said, "Are we going to have a sensible conversation now?"

Ella shrugged, but said nothing.

"Does that mean yes or no?" he asked.

She shrugged again.

"You said to me last night that we would talk after you'd seen your dad. I know you've seen him, so why aren't we talking?"

Ella realised that her mother and father would've spoken to each other and that her mother would've told her grandad. So he knew about the affair. But her mother wouldn't tell him about it over the phone so he had to have known before today. If so, why hadn't he told her? Now, even her granddad was lying to her. She shot him a venomous glare. "You knew she was having an affair."

Harry nodded slowly. "I did. Your mother told me only recently, although I had my suspicions."

"Then why didn't you tell me?"

"I wanted to," he said, "but your mother wanted to do things her way."

"You lied to me Grandad."

Harry reached out for Ella's arm. She tried to pull away, but he held it firmly.

"I did not lie to you," Harry said evenly. "I told you weeks ago that I wouldn't say anything about any suspicions I had until they were confirmed. This is a delicate situation, Ella, and it had to be talked about properly. Your mother should've told you herself. This is the situation I was trying to avoid."

He released her arm.

Ella realised her grandad wasn't responsible for the situation and was trying his best to mollify her without resorting to lies and half-truths. He looked pale and old. He didn't like what was going on any more than she did, but he had to live with it. Grandad was a sensitive and caring old man. She flung her arms around his neck. She sobbed, her body shook.

Harry hung on and wrapped his sympathy around her. The emotional traumas of the last few weeks were taking their toll on him.

After a few minutes, Harry freed himself from Ella and said, "I told your mother I'd ring her if you came here."

"I don't want to see her," Ella said.

"You can't avoid things all your life, especially big issues like this."

"I know, Grandad, but I'm staying at a friend's house tonight and I don't want to be upset any more than I am now. I'll see her tomorrow."

"I'll still have to tell her you're here. What she does is up to her. If she wants to come here and see you then I can't stop her. Do you understand?"

Ella nodded.

"Ok then, Tuppence. Make yourself something to eat and I'll ring your mother."

Ella went into the kitchen and heard her grandfather talking to her mother. He reassured her that Ella had calmed down and confirmed that permission had been granted for her to stay at Hannah's house that night. Arrangements were made for her mother to come over tomorrow afternoon.

In the kitchen, Harry said, "I've talked to your mother. She's coming over tomorrow. Your dad's coming as well. You'll all be able to sit around and talk it over."

"But you'll be there, Grandad, won't you?" Ella asked.

"If I'm invited to, yes," Harry said.

"I want you to be there, Grandad. I don't want to be in the middle of a fight between Mum and Dad."

"Ok, Tuppence." Harry smiled. "I'll be in your corner and act as referee." He smiled, but added more seriously, "I don't know the ins and outs of what's happened, but I think they've had a chat and come to some sort of agreement. I don't think there'll be any fighting tomorrow."

"I hope not, Grandad. It's awful to see two people you love fighting each other." She looked away wistfully. "I know things will never be the same again."

Harry kissed her on the cheek. "Time moves on," he said, "and drags us along with it. Your parents might not love each other but they both still love you. Come on now, finish what you're doing and get your things together. I'll take you to your friend's house. You sure you're ok?"

"I'm ok," Ella replied. "Do you love me, Grandad?"

The biggest smile that had visited Harry for a long time broke across his face. "I love you more than anything in the world, Tuppence."

They hugged each other tightly, taking comfort from each other, until Ella scampered away to her bedroom to get ready. Half an hour later, Harry drove Ella to Hannah's house and dropped her off.

Harry had taken half a loaf of bread to feed the ducks in the park – his second visit in a day. He parked the car and walked to his favourite bench. He sat there and fed the ducks and the swans and the pigeons and one or two itinerant seagulls that'd strayed inland. He sighed and watched the setting sun. It was peaceful here; the outside world rarely intruded. He relaxed and felt himself almost dozing off. Reluctantly he got up and started towards the exit before realising that he'd brought the car. He turned and walked the other way.

Soon he was back home reading the local newspaper in his

conservatory. His eye caught a story that said part of the High Street was going to be knocked down for redevelopment, and several premises, including charity shops, were closing. One of them was where Katrina worked. Either she didn't know or she hadn't told him.

He put the paper down and wondered how that would affect the relationship between Katrina and Will. Could it be that they'd split up? He shook his head. Their relationship was too involved. Something as trivial as Will losing his job wouldn't stop their inexorable fascination with each other. There were far too many other, more serious, problems to overcome. This was just a fly in the ointment.

***

Later that night, Harry was sitting watching television when the phone rang.

"Hello?" he said.

"Dad, it's me," said Katrina. "Ella's in trouble."

Harry's chest tightened instantly.

"What's happened?" he said.

"I've just had a phone call from Alison, Hannah's mother. She's returned home from her Bridge club to find Ella drunk. She rang me, but I'm about fifty miles away …"

Harry's eyes closed and he shook his head. Another night of passion with Will no doubt.

"… I need you to go and get her for me, Dad. Will you?"

Harry was already on his feet.

"I'll go right away. I'll ring you later," he said.

"I'll be there as soon as I can.

"No, Katrina. That's probably the worst thing that you can do," Harry said forcefully. "I'll look after her until she's better. We don't want things getting out of hand."

"Ok, Dad," Katrina said softly. "Text me when she's home."

Within ten minutes, Harry was bundling Ella into the car. She wasn't as bad as he had feared. She was slurring her words and was unsteady on her feet, her skin was burning hot and she was protesting her right to drink alcohol if she wanted to, but he'd seen worse. Occasionally she would squeal and cry. Harry managed to get her home and put her to bed fully clothed. He knew from experience that a bucket and face cloth were necessary accessories to a large bottle of water. The old remedy of drinking lots of coffee to sober up was hogwash as far as he was concerned. The only way to prevent a hangover was to drink water to keep hydrated.

He managed to get Ella to drink almost a pint of water before she threw up into the bucket. He wiped her face and gave her more water, despite her protestations. She threw up once more before she settled down and dropped off to sleep. Harry emptied the bucket down the toilet and washed it out before returning it to Ella's bedside, just in case. He dragged a chair into the bedroom and brought the duvet from his bed to wrap around himself. He'd sleep in the chair and be on hand, just in case.

He sent a text to Katrina to tell her that Ella was safe and sound in bed. He received a two word response: *Thanks Dad xxx*. He could almost feel her remorse through the phone.

He sat back and watched Ella sleeping. He'd thought she was handling things well, but today's events had proven that she was suffering more than he'd thought.

Ella woke up a couple of times through the night to go to the toilet. She didn't throw up again, but Harry made her drink water every time. She'd changed into her pyjamas and lay snuggled up, breathing deeply, with the occasional snort.

Around four in the morning, Harry stretched and took his duvet back to his bed. He lay for a few minutes mulling over the previous day then drifted off into a restless sleep.

***

Ella was up early.

Harry heard the stairs creaking as she made her way down them. He waited until he heard switches being turned on and the kettle being filled before he ventured out of his room, donning his dressing gown on the way.

Ella sat at the table with her head in her hands. When Harry entered the room she glanced up at him. "Morning, Grandad. Do I look as rough as you?" she asked.

His answer was straightforward. "Worse."

They both took time to pull themselves together – neither volunteering to enter into a conversation. They ate breakfast thinking their own thoughts.

The rattle of the letterbox caused them both to jump and they looked at each other with embarrassed smiles that grew into titters, then Ella started laughing. Harry saw the funny side of it and started to laugh out loud as well. Within moments they were both laughing uncontrollably, tears forming at the corner of their eyes. A few minutes later Harry reached out and held his granddaughter's hand. She rested her head on his forearm. With his other hand, Harry carefully pulled Ella's hair away from her face.

"You ok?" he asked her.

"Yes, Grandad. I'm sorry," she said.

"It's forgotten," he said. "It happens to us all sooner or later. Your mother was worried."

"Then why didn't she come for me?" she asked.

Harry considered the question. Was that what this was all

about? Did she want her mother to demonstrate how much she cared by coming to her aid when she was in trouble?

"Your mother asked me to go because she was too far away and thought I could get there quicker. And she was right. I said I would deal with it, and that we'd talk about it today."

Ella lifted her head. "Where was she?" she asked.

Harry shook his head. "I don't know, Tuppence."

"Was she with him," she said screwing up her face in contempt.

"I don't know that either," he answered, although she was probably right.

Ella put her head back on her grandad's forearm.

Silence reigned for a long time, until Harry moved his arm to wring out the pins and needles, and Ella sat up as if startled awake.

"We'd better get washed up, showered and dressed before your mother gets here," Harry said slowly. "Let's not give her anything more to worry about. Why don't we tell her that you did a little bit of experimenting and it got out of hand because you had a reaction to it, eh? You don't need to undergo a grilling from your mother, do you?"

She smiled at him. Grandad knew how to deal with things. If her mother saw her fresh and well, she'd think that it was a bit of a mountain out of a molehill reaction by Hannah's mother, and she wouldn't delve too deeply.

"Ok," she said as she disappeared upstairs to the shower.

***

Katrina arrived shortly after nine o'clock, well before the time she'd told Harry she'd be there, and let herself in. She obviously wanted to make sure Ella was alright. She found her father and daughter playing cards to pass the time. Both of them appeared to be in good humour.

The smell of freshly ground coffee made her hungry. She'd deliberately missed breakfast at the hotel. She'd stayed the night with Will, but it had turned from a romantic interlude into an argument. The world was falling down around her head and all he was interested in was having sex. When she'd left the hotel, Will was still in bed. He was going to go down to breakfast later. He'd waved a sleepy goodbye, which had annoyed her.

Katrina said in a jaunty voice, "Morning. And how are we all today?"

"We're fine," said Harry.

Ella smiled a broad, false smile and said, "I'm beating Grandad at cards."

Katrina's brow furrowed.

Harry noticed and said, "Ella had her first taste of vodka last night and had a bit of a reaction to it. As you can see she's fine now. There's nothing to worry about. I don't think she'll be doing that again in a hurry. Fancy a coffee? It's that nice Brazilian blend you like."

Katrina was surprised. She'd expected Ella to have a hangover. Alison must've exaggerated how drunk she was … if indeed she was even drunk. She adopted a motherly tone and said, "Now you know how it feels to act like an adult."

Ella kept the false smile and cheekily said, "Oh, I don't know about that. I've not had sex yet."

Harry glanced over his shoulder. Katrina's face was a picture. Harry suppressed a snigger and nearly swallowed his teeth.

"Ella!" Katrina said, "Don't be disgusting."

"I'm not the one being disgusting, Mother." Ella's smile had left her and been replaced by a look bordering on a sneer. "Where were you last night? Being disgusting with Will?" She spat out his name.

"Ella!" said Harry disapprovingly, "that's not how I would expect you to behave with anyone, never mind your mother."

He glared at her and she got the message.

"I'm sorry, Mum," she said, "that was mean of me."

Katrina regarded her daughter. She didn't know how to handle her these days. Her flashes of temper bore the hallmark of her father. He had a habit of blowing up over little things and apologising immediately. She simply nodded and said, "I'll have that coffee, Dad. Could I have a slice of toast? I haven't had any breakfast this morning."

Ella gave her a filthy look but curbed herself from making a snide comment.

Harry made some more coffee and a slice of toast for Katrina.

Later, in between bites, Katrina mentioned that Oliver would be coming at ten. Ella, feeling a little nervous about the meeting, said she had an upset stomach. She took some antacid solution to ease the symptoms and Harry suggested she lie down until her father came.

"How is she?" asked Katrina when she'd gone.

"She's ok," said Harry. "Don't talk to her about last night. I think she realises she was daft. What you've got to worry about is why she did it in the first place. Now fill me in about what happened yesterday."

She told him everything.

Harry listened in silence. He thought that *he'd* had a hell of a day. Now he realised that Ella's day had been much worse.

Katrina ended her story by describing the agreement that had been reached between herself and Oliver.

"I know it's not much of an agreement, Dad," she said, "but we all have to be honest with each other. Will and I plan to be together. This is for Ella's sake."

Harry said, "Don't kid yourself, Katrina. This is the best

solution for you and Will. This is not about Ella. Of course I'll look after her as best I can, but she's fifteen, she needs her mother now more than any other time. The way she sees it is that you're behaving like a lovesick puppy. She thinks you're behaviour is embarrassing."

Katrina seemed to shrivel into the chair. "I just want a life," she said quietly. "Is that too much to ask? I never wanted to hurt anyone."

Just then the front door bell rang.

"That must be Oliver," said Harry, moving into the passage.

Harry opened the door and a fresh-faced Oliver stood there with a couple of teenage magazines in hand. He'd had a haircut and tidied himself up a bit since Harry had last seen him.

"Morning, Harry. You're looking well," he said as he crossed the threshold and walked along the passage. He stepped into the living room, exaggerating shock when he saw Katrina. "Christ Almighty! What's the matter with you?" he said in his own belligerent way.

Harry interjected. "I think we're all feeling a little raw, that's all."

He held up a mug to Oliver and raised an enquiring eyebrow. Oliver shook his head and sat down. Ella walked in steadily and kissed her father in greeting. Oliver gave Ella the magazines.

For Harry it was a graphic indication of whose side she was on if push came to shove. He took the chair. "Ella's asked me to be here. Any objections?"

There were none. Everyone expected Harry to be there anyway. After all, he was the one tasked with looking after Ella in the short term.

Mainly for Ella's benefit, Harry outlined the compromise

reached between Oliver and Katrina. It was an acknowledgement that their life as a family was over. Ella remained sullen throughout. Katrina looked out of the window and Oliver gazed into the fireplace. Harry finished off and invited comments. None were forthcoming.

He sat down heavily in his chair and muttered, "I've said my bit. We all know where we stand now."

There was a few moments silence before Ella said, "I think we've got to be grateful for Grandad for being here. He's the one who's had so much dumped on him and who has the least amount of say in what happens."

It was a remarkable insight for such a young girl and Harry was proud of her. Katrina gave Oliver a look that revealed her shame, as well as her pride in their daughter. Oliver was completely nonplussed by it all.

Katrina cleared her throat. "I know I've caused all this. I'm sorry, I really am sorry." She turned to Ella and said, "I'm sorry for you, Ella. I can't begin to understand how you feel about me. Please don't hate me. I love you just as I always have done and there'll always be a place for you with me. I've not discussed a divorce with your father yet, but that's what I want."

Tears were streaming down Katrina's face. She was humbling herself and baring her soul at the same time. Raw emotion enveloped her. Twenty years of a relationship had been swept aside in a few seconds.

Ella was softly sobbing and Harry had a huge lump in his throat. Oliver continued to stare into the fireplace.

Oliver seemed to suddenly realise it was his turn to say something. He stood up, because it made him feel more authoritative. He coughed and held the lapel of his jacket like a politician.

"I'd like to say that none of this is my fault ..." he said in a loud, parliamentary voice.

Harry and Katrina shook their heads in tandem, both fearing another diatribe. Oliver saw their gestures and hastily moved on.

"… but I'm willing to admit that there are faults on both sides …"

Katrina looked at her father, surprised, and Harry returned the look. This was a first, Oliver admitting some culpability, albeit reluctantly.

"… My concern is for Ella. I must thank you, Harry, for looking after her. I'm sure you'll do a better job than you did with Katrina …"

Harry shook his head again. Oliver never failed to make himself look like a prat.

"… Katrina, we need to discuss the terms of any divorce before we let solicitors loose on our finances. There, I've said my bit."

He sat down.

Ella stood up and said, "I'm going back to bed," and left without saying goodbye.

The meeting had been brief. What was there left to say? The marriage was over. They'd virtually announced their intention to divorce. Awkwardness hung heavily in the air until both Katrina and Oliver could stand it no longer and left to contemplate their positions, although they were civil enough to agree to meet in two days' time, on Monday.

Harry felt desperately tired, and it was only eleven o'clock. Hazel would be at the funeral now, he thought. Sometimes the world was an awful place.

14

The rest of the day drifted aimlessly towards its end. Ella resurfaced after a couple of hours and consumed a tin of tomato soup, then retired to her room again. No mention was made of the previous night's adventures or the morning's détente with her parents. Cordiality appeared to be the order of the day.

Harry went for a walk with a bag of bread and popped into the park to greet Mistress Duck and her friends. The visit was short-lived but soothing. Perhaps the raw sensitivity of the past twenty-four hours had taken its toll, and Harry, like everyone else, was applying balm to his emotional wounds.

He hadn't heard from Hazel despite him sending her a text late in the afternoon. He was a bit concerned, until he remembered she had a hospital appointment. He frowned. He'd missed the significance of that remark. Did she mean she had a doctor's appointment at the hospital or an appointment for treatment at the hospital? He couldn't remember.

Harry felt as though he needed some significant indulgence to make him feel normal again. He went to the fish and chip shop and ordered cod, chips and mushy peas, liberally covered with salt and vinegar. He took it home and consumed it with two slices of crusty bread and butter, and a can of beer.

When Ella came downstairs, Harry was sitting in his

chair on the verge of sleep. Her entrance startled him and he scrambled upright. She gazed over the detritus of the meal and raised an eyebrow.

"You've been having a good time, Grandad," she said.

"It was delicious," he acknowledged. "I'm completely stuffed. I'll pay for that later. You said you didn't want any when I texted you."

"Too much grease for me," Ella said, scrunching her face as she left for the kitchen.

Harry cleared away his dishes and followed her.

Ella made herself a sandwich and opened a packet of crisps. She selected a bottle of flavoured water from the fridge and went back into the lounge to curl up on the sofa. Harry washed up and ambled ponderously back into the room to resume his place next to the fire.

"Had any thoughts about today?" he asked, more in hope than in expectation.

Ella munched on her sandwich, then said, "No, not really." She paused then said, "Shit happens."

Harry chose not to address the comment.

"I'm not the first, and I certainly won't be the last, person to be deliberately orphaned by their own parents," she continued.

Again, Harry chose not to address the inaccuracies of that statement. Instead he asked, "So, how do you feel about what happened today?"

"I don't really know," she said. "It hasn't really sunk in yet. I've been thinking about it all day, but I still can't work out what'll happen in the future. I presume these things take time. I have a friend at school whose parents have been getting a divorce for over two years. They can't agree on anything and it's going to court."

"Every divorce has to go to court to get a decree nisi and

then a decree absolute," Harry said. He saw the confusion in her face. "It's a legal process," he explained. "A Judge is told what the problems are between two people who no longer want to be with each other. The Judge asks whether or not things can be sorted out between them and asks them to see advisors. If they still can't come to some arrangement, a decree nisi is issued. After about six weeks, a decree absolute is issued and stamped by the Court. That's when the people become divorced."

"It's complicated isn't it?" Ella said.

"It certainly is if the two people involved don't agree with what each other are saying, or there's lots of money involved, and especially if there're kids. The law puts the interests of any children as its primary concern. After all, it's not their fault that their mother and father are divorcing. Whichever way it goes, it's a messy business," concluded Harry.

"Will I have to choose which parent to live with? Ella asked. An apprehensive look shrouded her face.

"It may come down to that," admitted Harry. "If you were much younger, the law would probably award custody to your mother. They prefer children to be with their mothers rather than the fathers."

"So I'm treated like a bit of property. I'm awarded to one person and not another," she said.

"It's not quite like that, Tuppence," said Harry trying to soften the tone. The Court has to make a decision in your best interests. It has to make someone answerable for your welfare and future. That's a serious responsibility."

Ella finished off her meal and sipped her water. She was obviously thinking things through for the millionth time that day, but was now considering the new information. After a while she said, "I wonder what'll happen in the future."

Harry didn't reply, but thought it better not to know.

Later that night, as Ella wearily climbed the stairs to bed she said, "Will you tell me a story, Grandad?"

"You thought that the last one I told you was poor, but I said that there might be more to come. There've been some developments in that one. I could finish it off."

Her brow furrowed. "Developments? Ok then. Let's hear how it goes."

"Give me a shout when you're ready," Harry said.

Ten minutes later Ella called out to her grandad and he came trooping into her bedroom and sat on the bed. "Can you remember what happened last time? he asked"

"Inkarta lived with her family and loved her husband and daughter. She also loved Estraneo, but told him she wasn't going to leave her husband for him. But then she changed her mind ... again. "

"Ok, then. This is how it finishes."

***

Rivelo was glad things were getting back to normal. The unpredictable nature of Inkarta was causing him a great deal of stress that he didn't need. Did she not recognise that he had an important position that demanded loyalty and unflinching support from his wife? He thought about Fanio, a woman who he met regularly through his work. She was attentive, loyal and extremely supportive. She was attractive and always smelled nice. Rivelo smiled. He'd ask Fanio her opinion about things.

Lela was a bit concerned. She'd noticed that her mother and father weren't getting on together but didn't know what to do about it. Perhaps it would all blow over and things would return to normal. Last week she'd been so upset she'd done a very foolish thing. Neither of her parents knew exactly what happened and she wasn't going to tell them the details although both knew something was wrong.

Inkarta tried her best at whatever she was doing but it never seemed to do any good. She planned family events inside the castle and day trips outside the castle, but neither Rivelo nor Lela carried the same enthusiasm for them. She felt that the world wasn't a happy place without the presence of Estraneo.

Several weeks passed and Estraneo went about his business on the stall. Inkarta didn't visit, but a new, regular visitor to the stall was Zelda. She told Estraneo who she was and he recognised her name as a friend of Inkarta. She kept him informed about what Inkarta was doing and the moods she was in. Estraneo formed the opinion that Inkarta was unhappy in her life without him, and was trying to live her life for the sake of her husband and daughter. He would wait.

One day Lela went to the village and was passing a shop of refreshments when she glanced in the window to see her father with a woman. She went into the crowded shop and stood next to them.

Rivelo said, "This is my friend, Fanio."

Fanio smiled and shook Lela's hand in greeting. Lela hadn't been there very long when Inkarta unexpectedly walked in and saw Lela with Rivelo and Fanio. She put her hand to her mouth in shock.

Rivelo came to her and said, "This was not planned."

Inkarta realised everyone was looking at her, and she didn't know what to do. From the corner of her eye she saw an arm waving at her. She looked, and saw Estraneo at another table. It was all too much for Inkarta and she fainted. After a few moments, Inkarta opened her eyes and saw everyone standing around her. They had worried looks on their faces.

She got to her feet and addressed them.

"The people who are important in my life are here. I have some things to say to you all."

They stood, eager to hear her words.

"I love Lela and I want her close to me. I no longer love Rivelo and I do not wish to live with him in our castle. Perhaps Fanio will take my place." Inkarta turned to Estraneo and said, "I love Estraneo and I want to be with him."

Estraneo smiled, as did Fanio. Rivelo didn't smile but didn't object either. Lela was the only person who was unhappy. The look on her face remained with her for a long time. Eventually, though, the smile returned when she saw her mother and father were happy again.

And Lela grew up to be a fine young woman in a world that was an exciting place to live.

***

Ella frowned and said, "That's a strange and sudden ending. What's that all about?"

Harry grimaced and looked away. "That's the best I can manage under the circumstances," he said. "Things could change again."

"How do you mean?"

Harry looked thoughtfully at his granddaughter for a long moment before saying, "Don't you think the story is a bit familiar, Tuppence?"

"Familiar?" Ella said, "but you made it up didn't you?"

"I did," Harry said, "but it was based on real people." He raised his eyes theatrically and nodded at her.

Ella was perplexed for a moment, then it came to her like a lightning bolt. She gasped in surprise. "It's me? I mean us? I mean Mum and Dad?" she spluttered.

Harry nodded slowly and confessed to the deception. "I built the story around what I thought was going on at the time, and then a little later, when I knew something was happening, I changed some events to fit."

Ella was speechless.

Harry went on. "The names of the characters are anagrams of the real people except for Zelda. I thought you would've guessed before now." He saw Ella mentally unscrambling the names. "Estraneo is Italian for stranger, I didn't know who he was until recently."

Ella lay quietly. She felt a little foolish for not having realised what the story was about, but maybe she had wanted to forget the real world so hadn't made the connection. Now it was obvious. Her mind recalled and picked over the story. No wonder it appeared to be haphazard and unfinished.

"The dark cloud makes sense now," she said to her watching grandfather, "and Inkarta finding work on a stall. I suppose the meeting Inkarta went to with Estraneo was Mum going away with her boss to the conference." She bit her lip and nodded in agreement with her own interpretation of events. She didn't want to contemplate her mother having sex with another man, especially on a regular basis. It was a disgusting thought. After a few moments she said in a whisper, "Are you saying that this is the way it'll all turn out? Is this the 'and everyone lived happily ever after' bit?"

Harry sighed and stroked her hair. "I don't know, Tuppence. All I know is that time marches on and people move on through all kinds of adversity. Some people say it's character forming. We are who we are and we react to whatever we experience. I've said before there's no right way and no wrong way. As you said earlier, and don't quote it back to me, shit happens and you've got to deal with it. There's a poem by a man called Henry Wadsworth Longfellow called *The Rainy*

Day that puts things into perspective. Do you want me to say it?

Ella nodded.

Harry had learnt it at school and been struck by its relevance to life in general. His father had quoted the poem on several occasions when there was a crisis of some sort. He cleared his throat and spoke.

The day is cold, and dark, and dreary;
It rains, and the wind is never weary;
The vine still clings to the mouldering wall,
But at every gust the dead leaves fall,
And the day is dark and dreary.

My life is cold, and dark, and dreary;
It rains, and the wind is never weary;
My thoughts still cling to the mouldering Past,
But the hopes of youth fall thick in the blast
And the days are dark and dreary.

Be still, sad heart! and cease repining;
Behind the clouds is the sun still shining;
Thy fate is the common fate of all,
Into each life some rain must fall,
Some days must be dark and dreary.

Harry finished the poem and smiled. Ella dabbed a tissue at the corners of her eyes.

"Although it doesn't seem so at first, I think the main theme of this poem is hope," Harry said genially. "Longfellow is saying that behind every problem we encounter, there is hope and sunshine; in other words, that every cloud has a silver lining; and every drop of rain brings a rainbow. And he's right.

It's just bloody difficult to bear at times."

Ella said, "I feel so sad, Grandad. I can't feel optimistic about the future at the moment."

"I know, Tuppence. But you can feel glad that there is a future for you. If your mother is happy with this Will guy, and your dad finds happiness with someone else, then who are we to question what they're doing. We've got to accept that they have the right to do it, and they've got to accept that we're not too happy about it. Will the ends justify the means, I wonder?"

Ella curled up tightly and looked like the little girl who had first stayed at her grandad's house when her parents had announced their separation weeks ago.

"Can I go to sleep now, Grandad? I'm very tired."

Harry got up and kissed her goodnight. "Nite nite, Tuppence," he whispered.

She didn't reply. She was already staring far away into the future and needed some time to adjust to her new horizons.

Harry went downstairs to make some tea and devour some antacid preparation; his meal was demonstrating its latent power over his digestive system. As he reached his chair, his mobile phone announced a message with the sound of a submerged submarine. It was from Hazel. It said: *Service was OK. Everything at Hosp OK. Hope you had a nice day.*

He smiled. He was glad for Hazel that it was all over and she could get on with her life. He'd tell her about his day the next time he saw her. It'd been a momentous day in both their lives. He sent a text to Katrina and Oliver to say that he'd spoken to Ella about their pending divorce.

Katrina replied with *Thanks Dad XXX.*

Oliver didn't reply. He was probably too busy.

Harry locked up and switched off the lights before heaving himself into bed. He lay there and thought about the day's events, but he never sorted them out because soon he was asleep.

Ella tossed and turned in her sleep. Vivid dreams punctuated her subconscious and occasionally caused her to wake up. It wasn't until the early hours that exhaustion overcame her. She slept well beyond breakfast time.

15

Katrina was a worried woman. Not only did she have problems with Ella, but Will had told her about the shop closing down for a redevelopment project. It meant that she'd no longer have a place of work, although she didn't need an excuse to go to work anymore. Will would probably be relocated, or a worst case scenario would mean he'd have to find another job elsewhere.

It was a problem she didn't need. She was fortunate to have her dad there to look after Ella, but if she were to divorce Oliver then she'd have to sell the house and find a job for herself. Oliver would provide maintenance, of course, but she wouldn't have the standard of living she was used to. What she didn't know was Will's financial status. He appeared to be reasonably well off, but they hadn't really discussed the whys and wherefores of co-habitation, including where they would live. She hadn't actually told him she was getting a divorce, and she made a mental note to ring a solicitor for an appointment soon. She didn't want to have a meeting with Oliver without some progress having been made in that direction. All in all, she had a lot on her plate.

Today was Sunday, and Katrina knew that Will would be at the shop for four hours by himself over the lunch break.

She readied herself and drove there, parking in the same place she'd been when Ella had seen her with Will the other day. She walked in via the back door and found Will sitting on a chair next to the till. There were no customers in the shop.

He looked up as she entered and his smile lit up his face. He stood up to welcome her and she threw herself into his arms, much to his astonishment. He immediately feared the worst.

"What's the matter?" he asked anxiously.

"Just hold me, Will," she said. "I've asked Oliver for a divorce and I've told him we're going to be together. Ella knows, too."

Will held her close, a million things rushing through his head. He didn't know if he should be elated or sad, and that clash of emotions neutralised him.

The moment was broken by a customer entering the shop.

Will broke free and became the professional shopkeeper. Katrina wandered into the back room. She saw a new window had been installed. It had putty fingerprints around its edges. All the tiny shards of glass had been vacuumed up and the piles of clothing and bric-a-brac had been adjusted and relocated to give the office area a clean and functional appearance. It was incredible to think that this shop, and about twenty others, was going to be bulldozed into oblivion soon.

She heard the doorbell ring and Will saying goodbye to the customer, who hadn't bought anything. Will quickly came through to the back.

"So that's it, then," he said. "We can be together."

She smiled. That was typical of Will. If there was a job to be done then he got on with it. He would want everything to be sorted as quickly as possible. There was no need to hang around if the barriers were removed.

"In one way things have been sorted," Katrina said, "but in another, it's just the first step."

Will took Katrina in his arms again and said, "It doesn't matter how long it takes. You've decided you want to spend your life with me. I know the sacrifices you've made just to get to this stage have been enormous, but now that you've got me to hold your hand, we'll be able to take on the world. Together, we're unbeatable." He kissed her. "I love you so much. Will you marry me when all this is sorted?"

"We've a long way to go first. Let's see what happens."

It wasn't the answer Will wanted to hear but it would suffice for now. He'd wait forever if that's what it took.

Katrina disengaged from him and sat down at the desk. Will remained standing.

"We need to sit down and talk about the future," Katrina said in a quiet but strained voice.

Will could see the tension was getting to her.

"We need some time together to go through all those practical things that get missed when decisions like these are taken," Katrina continued, gazing at Will with moistening eyes. "Are we doing the right thing?" she asked.

"Yes," said Will in as decisive a tone as he'd ever used. It was commanding and authoritative, and spoke volumes for his conviction that they deserved each other. Not just because they were lovers, but because they were friends and soul mates, too. "Can you come away with me this weekend?"

Katrina glanced up at him suspiciously, checking to see if his thoughts were focused on unbridled passion or whether they were a pragmatic interlude to some tough decisions. She decided it was the latter, but no doubt a bit of the former would also be welcome.

"Yes," she said squeezing his hand.

The doorbell interrupted again and Will went scurrying

back to the business end of the shop uttering a hearty welcome to an unsuspecting customer.

Katrina reflected on the forthcoming weekend away. Her father would agree to look after Ella. After all, she was staying there anyway. A moment of doubt crossed her mind. She was making an assumption that her dad didn't have anything planned for himself. She guiltily recalled that Oliver and Ella had made similar assumptions about her in the past. It was one of the main reasons why she wanted to assert her own identity, yet here she was taking the same liberties. Surely, though, she was justified; these were unusual circumstances. Would her father agree? She didn't know.

Katrina left the shop an hour later, after Will had reserved a two night weekend break in a country manor seventy miles away. Near enough to home for an emergency, she thought, but far enough away to be able to pretend they were a comfortable man and wife escaping city life to enjoy the countryside. She rang her dad to see if he was home. He wasn't. She rang his mobile and he answered immediately. He was in the park feeding the ducks. Wasn't he always?

She told him of her plans to go away with Will for the weekend to sort out the small print of their future together and asked him if he could look after Ella. He said he would and even suggested that it was a good idea for her to "let off some steam".

She loved her dad so much. Why couldn't she have met and married someone like him. He was everything she wanted in a man. Oliver had been good, she had to admit, Will appeared to be better, but neither of them came anywhere close to her dad.

***

Harry sat on the bench in the park looking out over the lake. Mistress Duck and her friends had been fed and were rapidly losing interest in him and Hazel, who sat next to him, having arrived a few seconds before he took the telephone call.

He put away his mobile phone and said to her by way of explanation, "That was Katrina. She wants me to look after Ella this weekend while she goes away with the boyfriend to sort things out."

"Is that what they call it these days?" said Hazel, raising an eyebrow. "I remember going away for weekends myself for a 'sorting out', and there's you telling her to let off some steam! It's a bucket of cold water she wants more than anything."

Harry chuckled. Even the trauma of the past few days had failed to dampen her indomitable sense of humour.

"How'd it go yesterday?" Harry asked. It was a general question covering the two events she'd attended the previous day – the funeral and the hospital appointment.

"Do you mind if I don't talk about it, Harry," Hazel said softly, dismissing any conversation about either subject. "Perhaps some other day, when I'm used to it."

Harry raised his hands in acquiescence. "Anytime you're ready," he said.

They sat for a few seconds watching some swans submerge their heads in the water with their tails sticking up in the air.

"When was the last time you were away for a weekend, Harry?"

Harry thought for a moment and said, "Must be about seven or eight years ago. You?"

"I was thinking that the last time I was on holiday was six years ago. Fino and I went to Spain for a fortnight. We had a good time, even though it pissed down for a week."

Harry saw the memories dance across her face and light up her eyes. His own thoughts brought reminiscences to mind, too, and they both sat there for several minutes enjoying their recollections.

It was Hazel who spoke first.

"Harry, I'm going to ask you a question. You needn't answer it if you don't want to and you won't upset me if you say no."

"Ok," he said. "Fire away."

"Just sitting here thinking about holidays and good times made me think that it's bloody ages since I had a good time. Fino was a strong, loving, caring man, and I absolutely adored him. It was the most wonderful feeling in the world to wake up naked in bed with his arms wrapped around me. Talking about it now gives me goose bumps. It was lovely to feel the roughness of his stubble on my face, the hair on his chest. We used to lie like that for ages. I liked that better than the sex, though that was great as well. I would love to experience something like that again." She paused a moment and took a deep breath. "Would you spend a weekend with me? Can I wake up in your arms and feel special again?"

Harry couldn't believe what he was hearing. This lovely, wonderful woman was asking him to spend a weekend away with her. His first reaction was shock, followed by pride with a mixture of fear and a little embarrassment. He didn't know how to react. It showed.

Hazel said, "Sorry, Harry. I don't want it to be awkward for you. It doesn't matter. Forget I asked."

Another few minutes flew by before Harry spoke. "I've never been asked to spend the weekend away with anyone ever before. That's a first, and probably the last. I'll tell you what I'm thinking, Hazel. I'm a lot older than you."

"Age doesn't come into it," Hazel interjected.

"Ok. I'm not the man I was, if you get my drift."

Hazel laughed. "I'm not asking you to shag me to death,

Harry. I just wanted a little loving that's all."

Harry was relieved. He thought that a sexual relationship would put an end to any platonic friendship, and he valued Hazel as a friend more than anything else. He pulled his shirt over his paunch and said jovially, "My body's not the sculptured temple it used to be."

Hazel laughed again. "I'm not exactly a super model either."

Harry grimaced momentarily and scratched his chin. "You're a beautiful woman, Hazel. To be honest, I'm frightened that I might embarrass myself. Some parts of my body may develop a mind of their own."

Hazel chuckled mischievously. "I think I can handle that."

Harry was shocked again until he saw the look on her face. They both laughed out loud. The embarrassment factor was eliminated.

"You're quite special, Harry. You're the only person I know who I can trust. You wouldn't take liberties or abuse your position. You're not a threat," she said seriously. "The more I talk about it, Harry, the more I want to do it. What do you think?"

"I'm flattered," he said. "I have to admit I'm quite taken with the idea of a holiday. It's been a long time."

"Listen," Hazel said," to hell with the weekend, why don't we try for a week abroad, somewhere like Spain, for instance?"

Harry thought for a moment. It was a great idea and appealed instantly. The prospect of some foreign sun on his face was immediately desirable. The first doubt crossed his mind when he thought about Ella – who would look after her? The doubt was erased when he convinced himself that she wasn't his concern. Her mother would have to make other arrangements. Then he thought about how Ella would see it. He knew she'd think that everyone was abandoning her and passing her around like an unwanted Christmas present.

Hazel could see some inner torment.

"Having second thoughts are we?"

"No. No," Harry replied. "I'm just thinking about how Ella's going to react when I tell her I'm not looking after her and going away for a holiday."

"She's not your responsibility," Hazel reminded him. "Look, why don't I try a little magic on the internet and see what I can do?"

Harry thought that seemed like a good idea. It was pointless building up hopes only for them to be dashed because there wasn't anything suitable to be found.

"By the way, do you have any preferences?" Hazel asked. The mischievous expression had returned. "I mean destinations, of course."

Harry barely contained his mirth. She really was a tonic. The prospect of spending some time with her gladdened his heart.

"Anywhere does for me," he said.

They parted company with a friendly kiss. Harry felt elated. The best he'd felt for such a long time. He had a spring in his step as he made his way home.

***

Harry was having his evening meal with Katrina and Ella when Hazel rang him on his mobile phone.

"Hi, Harry," she said excitedly. "How does a week on the Costa Del Sol sound?"

Harry grinned. Her excitement was infectious.

Although they couldn't hear what was being said, Katrina

and Ella exchanged furrowed looks. Something was going on.

"Sounds absolutely marvellous," said Harry.

"It's a place called Benalmadena. It's not far from the airport and it's just south of Torremolinos."

It didn't matter to Harry. He'd heard of Torremolinos but not Benalmadena. All he knew was that it was in Spain.

"When do we go?" he said.

Katrina and Ella looked at each other again. The furrowed brows had changed to frowns.

"Next Monday," Hazel said. "A week today. I'll pay for it on my card, Harry, if that's alright with you?"

"That's fine," Harry replied. "Let me know how much I owe you. I'd better go and check my passport." Although he already knew that it was current.

Katrina and Ella's eyes widened.

"Ok, Harry. I'll ring you when it's sorted. *Adios amigo.*"

"*Hasta luego, senora!*" chuckled Harry, then put his mobile back into his pocket. He smiled at his open-mouthed daughter and his startled granddaughter and said, "I'm going on holiday to Spain."

"You're going on holiday? To Spain? Who with?" said Katrina who was absolutely dumfounded. "When?"

Harry took his time to formulate an answer. He hadn't figured out a reply as yet, and part of him wanted to say that it was none of their business, and of course that was true to a certain extent. He didn't need to ask permission from anyone and he certainly didn't need to explain his actions. He made himself comfortable.

"I'm going on holiday with Hazel," he said. "A friend of mine."

Katrina didn't know whether to laugh or cry. Her father had a girlfriend? Surely not! She shook her head violently. Please, God, no more stress, she pleaded silently. She stared at her father and said, "You're going to have to explain this, Dad."

Ella looked at her mother darkly as if to say 'you think you're stressed, what about me?'

Harry breathed deeply to compose himself.

"Some time ago I met a woman called Hazel in the park and struck up a friendship. I see her quite often for a chat and to feed the ducks. I've been to her place a few times and she's been here on a couple of occasions."

Incredulous faces gazed at him.

"Her husband's just died and she wants me to go away on holiday with her. Oh, and I said yes." He finished abruptly and waited for the astonishment to subside and the inquisition to begin.

"Her husband's just died? Oh my God!" said Katrina covering her mouth with her hand.

"She buried him yesterday," Harry said to clarify matters, although it only served to add to the confusion.

Ella slapped the table and stood up. "Adults! Why do they make things so complicated?"

Katrina glared at her. "Sit down, Ella. I'm trying to get to the bottom of this."

Ella sat. Katrina turned to her father.

"So you're going on holiday with a widow who's just buried her husband. A woman you met in the park. Tell me more, Dad."

Harry thought for a moment. "She lives on the other side of the park. She's probably three or four years older than you. She's a lovely woman. She's called Hazel O'Shea."

"Oh my God," said Katrina for a second time. "A woman young enough to be your daughter."

"Just about."

"Oh, Dad," said Katrina. She'd heard that old men

sometimes developed latent sexual tendencies towards younger woman, but not her dad surely.

Ella sat slumped in the chair. The thought of her parents having sex was gross enough but knowing that your grandad was having sex was repulsive. She groaned.

"I don't know why you're getting upset," Harry declared. "It's not as if we're together in a sexual way."

"So you've got separate rooms," Katrina said.

"No, I don't think so," Harry replied, then added cheekily, "She says she wants to wake up one morning naked, next to a loving, caring man. I guess that means me."

"Dad!" shouted Katrina.

Ella melted further into her chair.

Harry stood up. "I can't see what all the fuss's about," he said. "It's just two people going on holiday together because they like each other's company, and both could do with a bit of sun on their faces, that's all." He said pointedly to Katrina, "There's nothing wrong with that surely? It is ok, isn't it? I mean you're going away this weekend for a bit of a holiday, aren't you?"

Katrina glared at him. She hadn't told Ella yet.

Ella was suddenly alert again and sat up rigidly in her chair. "You're going away as well? What is it with adults? Why do they always have to slope off to hotels to have sex? It's disgusting."

"I'm not sloping off anywhere," retorted Katrina. "Will and I are going away for a few days to talk about our future."

"So there's not going to be any sex, then?" Ella asked.

Katrina hesitated.

"I thought so," Ella said defiantly. "You must think I'm a complete idiot."

Harry raised his hands to call an end to hostilities. Arguing like this never solved anything.

"Nobody is sloping off anywhere. People do things for a variety of reasons and they don't normally have to explain why they do them." He looked firstly at Katrina and then Ella for a longer moment. He had made his point. "But to be completely honest we are always trying to justify our actions. I have to admit that when Hazel asked me to go away with her I had reservations because I thought she might've been suggesting intimacy of some kind, but I asked her outright and that cleared the air. We're just two friends who want time together in pleasant surroundings. A holiday, it's just that, a holiday. We're going away to have some fun. God knows I could do with some of that."

He sat down.

Ella looked glumly at her Mother.

Katrina was mollified more than Ella appeared to be. Harry could see that Ella was thinking the whole world was rejecting her in order to steal a few moments of pleasure.

Harry's pocket buzzed silently. He glanced at the text and smiled. It read: *Holiday booked.*

"It's from Hazel," he said. "It's all sorted. I'm off to Spain next Monday."

16

Ella lay in bed and thought that the person who had coined the phrase 'Life is shit and then you die' was spot on. It couldn't get any worse. She was supposed to be preparing for exams, yet her parents were divorcing because her mother was having an affair, her father had taken to chasing women and her grandfather was going on holiday with a woman he'd met in the park.

How did they expect her to behave as if everything was ok when it simply wasn't? It was alright for her grandad to recite a poem about how things got better, but did anybody care about what she was going through? She doubted it.

She was surprised about her grandad going on holiday with a strange woman, though she giggled despite herself. She probably wasn't a strange woman at all, just a woman who was a stranger, to her. Her grandad wasn't inclined to rash decisions. He always thought things through and usually came up with something no-one else had even considered.

Her mother was a different story. She thought she knew her but every day, lately, she came up with some new surprise. Now she was going away to 'sort things out', and have a lot of sex, no doubt. She wondered what her mother's boyfriend was like. He was a man who worked in a charity shop, which didn't worry her at all apart from the embarrassment it would cause if they ever went out together as a family and her friends saw her.

Her mother wouldn't have given up everything she had for someone who was angry or aggressive, sloppy or miserly. He would have to be a caring and gentle man to capture her heart in the way it'd happened. She'd have to ask her mother to meet him properly. God knows what he thought about her. All he'd seen of her was as an angry brat throwing a brick through a window. She blushed. It'd been an uncharacteristic act on her behalf. She'd ask her mother to introduce them before they went away together.

***

Oliver lay in bed wrapped in the perfume that permeated the room. Fiona lay next to him, naked and satiated. It had been their first time together, and Oliver was in love again. He was trying to differentiate between the primeval passion of the moment and the more intellectually satisfying feeling you get when you make a connection with someone. What was that modern phrase? Oh yes, someone who ticks all the boxes. He couldn't remember the last time he'd lain in bed and thought about someone other than himself. It'd been a long time since he'd felt this way about Katrina. Certainly, he hadn't felt this way since he'd started to climb the promotion ladder, or maybe since the birth of Ella.

His life as he knew it was breaking up. He was meeting Katrina tomorrow to draw up a plan of action. He'd have to make a list of what he wanted and on what he was prepared to negotiate or compromise. Katrina would expect him to be compliant. He would, but he wouldn't be a doormat. He'd approach things in the business-like manner that he was renowned for. She would get a shock if she expected him to let her walk all over him. He needed to consolidate and safeguard his future. After all she only had herself to blame. Other than maybe a little bit of neglect, this wasn't his fault at all.

And now he had Fiona. She'd told him tonight that he was special. She was a divorcée, twice. Both of her husbands had neglected her in some way. The first, a tradesman of some description, had spent more time at the local social club than at home. The second, the tradesman's manager, had been happy working in his office and didn't seek further promotion. Fiona interpreted that as him not wanting to provide for his family, although they didn't have children. As a result of this obvious neglect, she'd been seduced by the firm's managing director and the marriage had broken up. She'd been forced to take a job elsewhere and landed a job with Oliver's company.

Fiona was special to him now. He could see in her eyes that she had love in them but she was afraid to say so. She was so vulnerable. Which wasn't surprising after all that had happened to her in the past. He decided to take her away this weekend – somewhere in the country.

***

Katrina lounged on the sofa with a cup of herbal tea in hand – camomile, to sooth her nerves and help her sleep, although it hadn't worked in the past few weeks. She'd spoken to Will and told him about the day's events. He'd laughed when she'd mentioned her father was going away with a lady friend she hadn't known existed until today. She couldn't imagine anyone thinking of her father as being some sexual athlete, or a gigolo, but it took all sorts, as her father was fond of saying. She'd asked Will to make a list of things to discuss over the weekend. He'd laughed again.

"A list? Why do we need a list? Everything's on it and

nothing's on it. There will be practical matters, of course, but all we need is a timeframe for things to take place. Starting today."

She'd tried to control his enthusiasm, but he was having none of it. They were going away on their first official weekend together and nothing was going to stop him from enjoying the experience. Katrina gave up and succumbed to the draw of the camomile tea to ease the worries.

***

Hazel lay in the bath thinking about Fino. She'd asked him in her prayers for his blessing to go away with Harry, although she felt as though he'd already given his permission. They'd had the same conversations every couple had about what they'd do if their partners died before them. They'd both agreed that life was for living – so go for it.

She remembered a phrase she'd heard on television some years ago, by someone who was trying to encapsulate the meaning of life. He'd said, "Life is just one long warm bath." She hadn't understood that at all, but now, lying in a warm bath, she appreciated the sentiment.

The aromatic waters leached the pain from her body and her mind, and replaced it with a soothing balm that nourished her soul. She smiled at the memory of Fino debating whether she should take a lover if anything happened to him. They'd made love afterwards, and it had been in one of those post coital naked embraces when she felt such moments of intense love that it moved her to tears. Moments like those were difficult to recreate, but the feelings of comfort and serenity could be recaptured in the arms of someone prepared to give themselves to another. She'd tried to explain this to Harry, although not very successfully. However, she felt as though he'd grasped the concept, and he'd agreed to the holiday. If it didn't work out then she'd not lost anything.

Reluctantly, she got out of the bath and dried herself before putting on her dressing gown. As she entered the bedroom, she picked up the holiday printouts and scanned them, feeling the excitement building again. It would be nice to have a holiday. She wandered over to the dressing table and picked up a photograph of Fino working at his desk. She'd often looked at the photo and wondered what he was thinking about when it was taken. He had a faraway look in his eyes that contained a bit of fear. It was as if he knew what his future held. She kissed him as she'd done every day since he'd been institutionalised, and whispered a soft, "Goodnight, love", before switching off the light and getting into bed.

***

Harry lay awake. He'd put down the book because he couldn't concentrate. There was so much going on. He was pleased to be going on holiday with Hazel, although he still had reservations about sleeping with her. He'd not slept with another person since Thelma had died and he'd forgotten about any protocols that might have to be observed with a new partner. He was sure there weren't any, but he wanted Hazel to have the wonderful experience she craved. He certainly didn't want to be the cause of why she couldn't have that experience.

He planned a trip to town – there were things he needed, like new underwear and a couple of leisure shirts. He'd need sunglasses, lotions and creams. Soon he'd built a sizeable list that he knew instinctively was too long. He decided to ring Hazel in the morning. She would be taking stuff and there was no use duplicating them, especially if there was a limit on the luggage allowance. He settled down and turned onto his side.

Soon he was asleep, dreaming of the sun, the sea and the sand he hadn't seen for a very long time.

17

Ella woke, after a comfortable night's sleep, with a fresh determination to stop being a permanent victim in other people's lives. She accepted her situation and that of her parents. As her grandad had said, she could accept it, but she didn't have to like it. It was pointless bleating about how her life had been ruined. She was still alive and healthy. She still had exams coming up that dictated her direction of future study, and within a few years she'd be at university somewhere. She'd still have two parents who loved her, and maybe a step-father and a step-mother to contend with. A part of her knew that she was dreaming of a perfect scenario and that real life might compromise that. Nevertheless, she'd approach life from a different angle and see what it brought.

She rang her mother and asked if she could meet Will. Katrina was guarded at first, but said she'd make arrangements to have lunch. She'd contact Ella later.

Harry was making breakfast at the time, and nodded his approval at Ella's initiative. "That was a good move," he said.

"Thanks, Grandad," Ella said. "I've decided I need to grow up fast. It's like you said, I've got my own life ahead of me and I need to make my own way. Mum and Dad can provide me with a good set of values to live my life, but I need to start making my own decisions for *my* future."

Harry saw the determination in her face. There was also a trace of fear. She was still young and although it was true that she'd have to make decisions about her life, she was, in his opinion, still too young.

He sat on a kitchen stool and adopted a philosophical face. "I can see where you're coming from, Tuppence," he said sagely, "but you must realise that you're bound to make mistakes from time to time."

He paused for thought.

"There's no harm in that as long as you learn from them. And you have to realise that there will always be support there if you need it. There's no need for you to dive straight into life, though. Dip your toe in the water and test it out. Go for a paddle, then wade in up to your waist. When you're used to it, try swimming, but never get out of your depth, because the tide can change at any time."

He was pleased with the metaphor.

"The most important piece of advice I can give you is this: beware of people. They can build you up and tear you down. Most people are good, but there are others who might want to harm you or see you fall flat on your face. The trouble is, you can't tell the difference."

He put his arms around her. "You're a good girl, Ella, a fine young woman. I'm so very proud of you."

Ella melted against her grandfather, on the verge of tears. It was a difficult transition to manage; this passage of growing from girl to woman was like no other. The physiological and hormonal changes themselves were epochal, never mind the psychological and emotional adjustments that had to be made.

Harry kissed his granddaughter and moved over to the toaster.

"Smells like the toast's burning," he said.

A few minutes later a text message from Katrina arrived, confirming lunch with Will.

"I'll give you a lift," Harry said. "I've got to go into town to get a few things for the holiday anyway."

Ella mockingly narrowed her eyes at her grandfather and said, "Yes, you need some protection." She waited for his questioning look before adding, "From the sunshine, Grandad, from the sunshine."

Harry blushed for the first time in many years and laughed, partly in embarrassment. "Which reminds me," he said, "I need to speak to Hazel."

He got up and made his way to the telephone.

Ella said, "Can I meet her, Grandad. Can I meet Hazel before you go on holiday?"

"You've already met her," Harry said. "Remember when you ran into the park looking for me after you'd smashed the window …?"

Ella nodded.

"… The woman you spoke to on the bench was Hazel."

Ella replayed the moment in her mind. "I remember her," she said in amazement. "She looked as if she'd been crying."

Harry nodded. "Well, now you know why she was crying."

Ella stared into her memory for a few seconds. "But that wasn't meeting her, Grandad. I mean, not a how-do-you-do type meeting. I would like to meet her for tea or something. I'm sure Mum would like that as well."

That was a reasonable observation, Harry thought. He'd ask her and see what she said. "Ok, I'll do that," he said, and moved off to make the call.

Ella sat and listened to her grandad talking to Hazel. He sounded excited and happy. She was pleased for him. He didn't have an awful lot of enjoyment in his life. Most of his pleasure came from within his family. That was good enough for him most of the time, at least until recently, so this was an unexpected pleasure in its own right.

Harry returned with a list in his hand. "Not as long as I thought it was going to be," he said. "Hazel's got most of what we need. Just a few odds and sods, really. Come on, then, Tuppence, let's get washed up and we'll be away."

Harry and Ella shopped for shirts, underwear and sunglasses. Ella played the role of Harry's technical advisor. He wanted something functional and traditional. She advised contemporary and cool – at least a grandad's version of contemporary and cool. She compromised on the underwear.

They were laughing together as Harry dropped Ella at the restaurant and they said farewell with a kiss. Harry drove away in a buoyant mood. He'd had fun with his granddaughter and he'd really enjoyed it. He glanced at the yellow-framed reflective sunglasses and doubts resurfaced. Then he remembered trying them on in the shop and recalled the spontaneous grin that had swept across his face.

He drove down the High Street and saw Hazel coming out of a chemist shop. He tooted his horn and pulled over. She came to the car.

"Going my way?" Harry asked.

"Not yet, Harry. I've got to collect some clothes from the dry cleaners, then I'm finished."

"In that case," Harry said, "I'll park the car and I'll meet you at Angelo's. I'm taking you to lunch."

"Wow," Hazel said, "now you're talking. Give me fifteen minutes."

***

Six o'clock chimed on the mantelpiece clock. Harry rubbed his eyes to stop himself falling back to sleep. He'd dozed since he'd come back home with Hazel – she needed his passport details to book the flights on-line. Hazel had walked home despite his protestations. She said she would go home via the park to make sure that Mistress Duck got the remnants of his dough balls and pizza. He'd already sent a text to Ella saying that he'd had lunch out and wouldn't be making an evening meal. She'd sent one back saying that was ok. He'd also asked if she was having a good time. She replied: *Absolutely fine lol.* He had no idea what that meant.

Katrina brought Ella home. The lunch had developed into a walk by the river and a soft drink in a pub.

"How's things?" asked Harry of no-one in particular.

Ella said, "Fine."

Katrina said, "Things went as well as could be expected in the circumstances. I'm very proud of Ella. I could see she was making an effort to like … er … to get on with Will, but there's still a long way to go."

"Good," said Harry. He waited a moment to see if anyone was going to say anything else, then said, "I've invited Hazel for tea on Thursday so you can meet her properly."

Katrina and Ella looked at each other conspiratorially, but they didn't say anything.

"Is that ok?" Harry asked, unsure what the exchange of looks meant.

"Yep," said Ella.

"I think so," said Katrina.

"Good," Harry said, raising his eyebrows. "I'll collect some doughnuts and custard slices from the bakers, unless you want something different?"

Both of them shook their heads.

A little while later, Ella went upstairs to her room.

Harry waited until the door had shut firmly behind her before saying to Katrina, "So how did it really go?"

"It went fine. Like I said, I was really proud of the way she behaved. She apologised for throwing the brick through the window and said that it was out of character. Will accepted the apology and told her that we'd all been a bit stressed out lately and that was affecting our behaviour. He stood up, said hello, and formerly shook her hand. He said that we should start from scratch."

Harry nodded his approval.

Katrina continued. "Will told her straight. He said that he loved me and we intended to set up home together."

Harry thought that a little bit premature given that they were going away this weekend to sort out their future. Perhaps some things had already been sorted.

Katrina went on. "He said that we would want her to live with us, but he understood if she decided on some other arrangement. There'd be no pressure from us." She looked steadily at her father digesting this news. "Dad ..." she said.

Harry could see where this was going. "I know," he said. "She can stay here as long as it takes. But I've told you before, Katrina, I'm her grandfather not her father. She's still a minor. I can't make decisions for her. I can only advise you, or her for that matter. She'll not want to stay with you until she gets to know Will better. She won't want to stay with Oliver because it would cramp his style. If you couldn't handle it then she wouldn't either."

He walked around the room. The implications of Ella staying there on a permanent basis were huge, but he couldn't see any practical alternative. However, if Ella's new maturity was maintained, it wouldn't affect him too much. But things could change at a moment's notice.

"Thanks, Dad," Katrina said. "I want Ella with me, but

I know it's too much to ask of her at the moment. Will and I need to make some plans. I've promised Ella that she'll be included in any discussions that impact on her."

"That's good," Harry said, "but you do realise that everything you decide impacts on her. You've also got to take into consideration that she may try to veto any decision you make, or try to sabotage them. She's trying hard to be adult about it, but she hasn't got the maturity yet to take any adverse decisions in her stride. There are also Oliver's wishes to consider. You never know what he's thinking."

"I know," Katrina admitted. "I'm seeing him tomorrow."

18

The meeting between Katrina and Oliver went by in a flash. Oliver defended his claims on all things domestic and insisted that everything should be split down the middle. He waved sheets of paper, copies of bank statements and details of family assets at Katrina and they both agreed to reject any overtures about reconciliation. The house would be sold, Katrina would keep her car and the monies in the bank accounts would be split 50:50. The crucial thing, from Katrina's point of view, was that she would have custody of Ella, as long as she admitted adultery in order to salve Oliver's bloated ego.

They agreed that Katrina would remain in the family home and supervise the sale of the house. They agreed that the level of maintenance should be argued by the solicitors. The talks were without acrimony or rancour and they parted on genial terms.

Katrina was filled with sadness when Oliver left the house with some belongings in a couple of green garden waste sacks. She felt an overwhelming feeling of failure despite her relative success at negotiations. The sense of failure was down to the marriage itself. Her hopes, dreams and ambitions had been destroyed, not by circumstances or anything beyond her control, but by her own actions. She had broken up the marriage because she'd fallen in love with someone else. She couldn't imagine what her reaction would be if someone said that to *her*. She resolved to ring the family solicitor the next day.

Oliver had also agreed to that. He was going to use someone he knew who was connected to his company.

Katrina rang Will and told him what had happened.

It was difficult for Will. He wanted to shout from the rooftops that he was going to live with the love of his life, but his response was muted because he knew Katrina was hurting. The time would come when they could celebrate their union without a care in the world.

Katrina rang her father and told him what had gone on.

Harry listened carefully without comment. He was pleased there was no animosity between them; any bad feeling would've had a negative impact on Ella. Ella needed to be able to relate to them both simultaneously without having to worry about allegations of betrayal or spying. The conversation finished with him reminding Katrina about tea with Hazel. Harry could almost feel her grinding her teeth on the other end of the phone.

Harry told Ella that her parents had met and it had been an amicable meeting.

"Who won first prize?" she said sarcastically, punching the cushion into shape so she could use it as a pillow.

Harry said, "If you mean who will have custody of you, then that's going to be your mother."

"Why can't you have custody, Grandad?"

He smiled. "I'm not your parent, although there's no legal reason why I can't. I think that the arrangement they've come up with is the best for you."

He clasped his hands over his paunch and settled back into his chair.

"Your mother is going to be living at your house until it's sold. That takes months. If you want to go back there, you can. If you want to stay here with me until everything is sorted out, you can. It's all in your hands, bearing in mind that when I go to Spain next week you'll be back with your mother anyway."

Ella wrinkled her nose. She was comfortable with Grandad, but she realised that her life was a lot more chaotic when she lived with him. All her things were back at home, so she'd be more comfortable there. She'd be with her mother, and her father was hardly ever there anyway, so there'd be less disruption. She frowned. A thought she didn't like visited her. If the road was clear, then presumably Will would be a more frequent visitor. Her mother might decide to allow him to stay the night, and that meant they'd be sleeping together. Ugh! The prospect of coming down to breakfast and finding Will and her mother having tea and toast in their dressing gowns was awful.

"Why don't you think about it, Tuppence, and let me know," said Harry.

"Ok, Grandad," she said. More things to think about. More decisions to make. The stress just keeps coming, she thought.

***

Hazel walked up the cul-de-sac to Harry's house for tea with the family. She saw a car parked next to Harry's and assumed it was his daughter's. Ella would already be there.

She hadn't made any special effort when dressing, although she already thought that her ordinary clothes were better than most people's best. She wore a simple plum coloured dress with deep purple shoes and matching handbag. As far as she was concerned they could take her or leave her. It wasn't as though she was asking for approval or anything. She was only being polite. Harry had asked her to tea to meet his daughter and granddaughter and she'd accepted. If there were any problems it would be theirs and not hers.

Harry opened the door for her before she'd knocked. He wore a big smile on his face and a nervous step in his legs. He kissed her on the cheek, led her silently into his lounge and introduced her to a woman slightly younger than herself who was sitting on the sofa with a fixed smile on her face, and, beside her, the girl she'd met briefly in the park, her face expressionless.

Hazel sat in a comfortable armchair and regarded the serious faces sitting opposite her. "Feels like a bloody interview," she said smiling.

Katrina's eyebrows shot up. Ella smiled. Harry chuckled.

"How many other candidates are there, Harry? I'd like to know what I'm up against. Apart from you, that is. If you get my drift," she said nudging him playfully.

Harry chuckled even more. Ella tittered. Katrina lowered an eyebrow.

"So where's this tea, then," Hazel asked as she placed her handbag on the floor. She winked at Katrina. "I quite like something sticky with mine, but the nearest I get to that with Harry is a custard slice."

Ella laughed and blushed at the same time. Katrina smiled politely. Harry disappeared into the kitchen laughing.

Hazel wasn't what Ella expected. The person she'd seen crying in the park was a different person to the funny, vibrant woman who was sitting in the armchair. She liked her instantly.

There was a brief pause while the two adult women eyed each other up, making assessments and judgements.

Ella said, "I like your dress, Mrs O'Shea."

"Well thank you very much," Hazel replied, "but please call me Hazel."

Harry carried in the tea tray and went back out for the cakes. He brought a cake stand Katrina hadn't seen for nearly twenty years that contained a variety of cakes and a few plates and knives.

"C'mon then, ladies, help yourself," Harry said.

"Wow," said Hazel surveying the fare, "you've really done us proud." She picked the stickiest cake on display and bit into it. Cream oozed onto her chin and it remained there until she'd finished chewing. She wiped it away with a finger and licked it clean.

Katrina nibbled at a Bakewell Tart while Ella and Harry wrestled with a custard slice.

"Well, this is nice," exclaimed Harry. Whether he meant the occasion or the cake wasn't clear but everyone ate and sipped tea.

Katrina said politely, "Dad tells me that you've arranged a nice little holiday for you both in Spain."

"That's right," Hazel replied. "It's a place called Benalmadena on the Costa Del Sol. I've been there before, with my husband. I got blind drunk there one day and burnt me arse with the sun. I couldn't sit down for three days."

Ella burst out laughing. So did Harry. Katrina froze in the act of biting into the tart.

"It could've been worse, though," Hazel continued. "I could've been lying on me back. I was naked you see."

Katrina tried to ignore the comment and compose herself. "Are you in a two roomed apartment?

"No, no, none of that," said Hazel, "we've got a double bed hotel room. We'll be able to snuggle up and rub each other with sun cream."

Ella suspected that Hazel was winding her mother up and

decided to join in. She said, "I hope you have a lovely holiday with Grandad. He deserves to have a nice time with a friend. My mum's doing the same this weekend with her friend." Her mother shot her a black look but Ella continued. "As a matter of fact, my father is going away with a friend this weekend as well. However, I think they have a different interpretation of what a friend is."

It was Hazel's turn to laugh, and Harry's smile was one of pride, not amusement. Katrina blushed.

Hazel looked Katrina straight in the eye and said, "Your dad and I have grown to be good friends. We're comfortable enough together to grant each other favours. I asked your dad to grant me mine, and he's agreed. We're two people alone in the world, and we respect and trust the values we live by. Your father's safe with me, and I feel safe with your father."

Katrina nodded guiltily. She'd been given answers to all her questions without even asking them. She mellowed visibly and the guarded atmosphere evaporated. "Would you like some more tea?" she said to Hazel.

"Thank you. I'll need some to finish off that chocolate éclair," Hazel said pointing to the second layer of cakes.

The conversation became more generalised and continued at a superficial level. No more mention was made of the holiday or weekends away. The subject of Fino's death was briefly brought up and sympathetic platitudes were exchanged. The revitalisation of the town centre became a topic of conversation and they discussed the impact this would have on jobs and shopping.

After an hour or so, Hazel said her farewells and left for home. Katrina's offer of a lift was politely refused – the ducks had to be fed *en route*. Harry nodded his approval.

"She's nice, Grandad," Ella said after Hazel had gone. "I think you'll have a good time with her. You'll have to ask her around again when you get back. That is if you're still speaking after you've been on holiday, of course," she added with a grin.

Katrina didn't make any comment about Hazel because she didn't want to be seen to approve the arrangement. She thought that Hazel was okay, but her father wasn't setting a good example for her daughter.

"Dad, as far as I can see, assignations such as this are simply wrong. Surely love must be involved somewhere along the line. Functional granting of favours, because that's what this is, when it involves sex without love, is improper and debases any loving relationship," she said loftily.

Ella leapt to her grandfather's defence. "Mum, take a look in the mirror and then listen to yourself. As far as I can see, Grandad and Hazel are being a lot more honest than you've been in the last few months."

Katrina was bewildered and stung by Ella's remarks. Harry remained impassive; his granddaughter had said it all.

Katrina picked up her handbag and took out the car keys. She said, "I have to go. I have an appointment with the solicitor and I need to calm down a bit before I see him." She gave her father and daughter a perfunctory kiss and left.

Harry sat down with Ella.

"I don't think your mother is too impressed with me," said Harry forlornly.

"She's a bit mixed up, Grandad, that's all. It's got nothing to do with her what you and Hazel do together."

Harry was learning about Ella every day; her new found resilience and detachment were a revelation to him. Her wisdom may be short lived, but it was very profound.

There was a brief silence which was eventually broken by Ella.

"Did you ever picture yourself as a stud, Grandad?"

Her words got the desired reaction. Harry's head jerked around in surprise, only to find Ella laughing. For a second or two he didn't know how to respond, then he burst out laughing at the improbability of the description.

"A stud? Me? I don't think so." He shook his head and laughed once more.

His thoughts, though, wandered. Duties as a stud weren't part of the holiday. It hadn't crossed his mind because it had never been part of what Hazel had called 'a favour'. But now that it had been said out loud, how would he react if it became an option while they were away? He didn't know.

***

Oliver put down the telephone. The call had been from Katrina saying she'd consulted with her solicitor and his advice was to sue for divorce on the grounds of irretrievable breakdown of the marriage based on Oliver's unreasonable behaviour, which meant his neglect of Katrina when he spent too much time at work. His own solicitor had suggested that that would be the likely scenario. Oliver wasn't happy. It was obvious in his eyes that any divorce proceedings should be based on Katrina's adultery and not anything he had done or failed to do. As he kept on telling people, none of this was his fault. His counsel's advice was not to contest the allegation as that would mean a more protracted divorce, more publicity and expense, and it would still have the same result. The deciding factor, as far as he was concerned, was that this route provided a clean break and less impact on Ella

"That was Katrina," he said to the blonde woman lying by his side.

"I guessed that," she said. She'd have to put up with his constant referrals to his soon-to-be ex-wife for a long while yet.

"You'll have to take it on the chin, Ollie." She was the only person who he'd granted permission to use his name in that way. "You'll soon be rid of her and we can start to be official."

He gazed over her naked body and once more felt the shiver of excitement stirring deep inside him. He stroked the inside of her right thigh. "I suppose so," he said. "I just feel a little bit frustrated that's all."

"Well, I think I have the cure for that," she said as she reached out and pulled him down to her.

Oliver surrendered, as he always did when Fiona was about. She was utterly irresistible. He had neither the power nor the desire to rebut her temptations. This weekend promised pleasures of bacchanalian proportions.

***

Will sat in an armchair with a large glass of red wine. He hadn't done much drinking and the wine had been heated by the warmth of his hand. He was deep in thought. The call from Katrina was a welcome interruption. Her progress with the solicitor and her discussion with Oliver had really galvanised him into thinking about his future with Katrina. He worried whether or not Katrina would marry him. She would almost certainly have deep concerns over the break-up of her marriage, and despite her protestations to the contrary, she would have second thoughts about getting married again. She might want to sample the life of a divorcée before settling down again. It was his biggest fear. But, perhaps that was down to his own insecurities. He was a born worrier.

The prospect of spending a whole weekend with Katrina was thrilling. Hopefully, she would rid herself of the inhibitions that had soured previous attempts to manufacture a romantic tryst. There were plans to make, of course. They had talked several times of a potential life together, but it had been based on wishes and hopes rather than solid, meaningful facts and figures. At the back of his mind he'd feared that it would always be a 'what if …' situation between Katrina and him, but now reality was knocking on his door.

He sipped some wine and then set the glass down on the table. He wasn't really in the mood for drinking

"A penny for them?" said his wife.

He smiled at her. "Sorry, I was miles away. I was just thinking about Katrina and the divorce, and the weekend away, and a million other things, too."

"Relax," she said. "From what you tell me, things are going along really nicely. Have some fun this weekend. When that's over, the hard work begins. You've still got a few problems – like building a relationship with Katrina's daughter. On top of that you've got to ask yourself where you're going to work when the shop closes."

It had been strange discussing his girlfriend with his wife, although the reverse had occurred a couple of times in the past when she'd had boyfriends.

Their love for each other was an early casualty of their marriage. They'd married too young, and before they'd realised that what they felt for each other wasn't love at all but a meaningful regard and respect, their chances of marital success were gone. They'd acted as man and wife until about ten years ago, but now lived as friends in the same house. Neither abused their new relationship, but there was an understanding that they would lead separate lives beyond the four walls. It had seemed contrived at first, but it soon settled down to a cosy brother and sister type relationship. Any sexual encounters with other people were discussed and celebrated for their own worth, just as friends would do.

The only thing that was a thorn in their sides was the

influence of the Catholic Church. Will was a Catholic by birth and nothing else. His wife was a practising Catholic with contemporary and pragmatic views, but his mother-in-law was a devout Catholic who espoused traditional beliefs. For her, divorce was a sin and could not be tolerated.

Will had explained his domestic situation to a doubting Katrina. She hadn't quite believed him until he'd engineered a meeting with his wife. Katrina and Maria had liked each other instantly.

"I'm looking forward to the weekend," he said. "We need to sort things out, as well as have some fun. The job …" he shrugged his shoulders, "...who knows. I'll cross that bridge when I come to it." He smiled at his wife. "Thanks for being there for me, Maria. Our conversations over the past few months have been really helpful. In some ways I'll be sorry to leave here. I'll miss you so much."

He got up and went to her. Their embrace was close and meaningful. Their respect for each other was manifest, and completely platonic.

19

Ella's newfound maturity didn't last beyond her parents' preparations for their respective weekends away with their new partners. The sullen Ella returned, to snipe at her mother and deride her father. She cried short of actually calling them names.

Harry knew what was going on. It was attention seeking at its most obvious. Her parents were going away to enjoy themselves and she was staying at home. He had no doubt that her mood would lift later in the day. He thought the vitriol would return on Sunday when her parents came home and he was about to fly to Spain the following day. Nevertheless, it was going to be a long weekend.

***

Oliver pulled up at the Country House Hotel and booked in. Fiona was radiant at his side. His daughter's histrionics had failed to dampen his ardour, and within fifteen minutes they were embroiled in a steamy romp on the four-poster bed. His initial plans for a swim and a sauna were abandoned.

***

Will and Katrina admired their room and their surroundings. A bouquet of flowers, a small box of bespoke chocolates and a bottle of red wine adorned the foot of the bed.

Will had decided he wasn't going to rush things. He was aware that Katrina needed to relax into the weekend after the verbal bashing she'd endured from Ella. He'd let her set her own pace.

It was a spacious room, albeit a bit chintzy. It overlooked a walled garden in full bloom at the rear of the hotel. The only blight to the ambiance of the place was the energetic sounds of someone making love in the next room.

Will smiled – someone was having fun and didn't care who knew it. Katrina either didn't recognise the primeval sounds or chose to disregard them.

Will poured a glass of wine for them both and opened the French windows. The soft, warm breeze stirred the curtains and wafted the scent of the flowers around the room. He gave Katrina her wine and kissed her lightly on the forehead. "To us," he said raising the glass to the outside world before sipping from it.

Katrina drank without endorsing his toast.

"This is the start we dreamed of," Will said. He kissed Katrina lightly again. "From today, nothing will stop us from being together ever again."

Katrina gripped his hand and squeezed it for all she was worth.

***

Oliver showered and shaved before donning the hotel's luxurious dressing gown. Fiona lounged in the bath soaking up the free bubbles.

It had been an energetic and frenetic fusion of limbs that had reminded Oliver of his teen years, when physical prowess, rather than technique, was regarded as the measure for sexual potency. He lay on the bed and reflected that perhaps the divorce was a good thing for him. He was sorry for Ella, but she would get over it fairly quickly. She would be leaving school and going away to university in a couple of years or so anyway. The divorce would only push that domestic schism forward a bit. If it hadn't been for Katrina doing the dirty on him, he wouldn't have found himself with Fiona.

He thought about Fiona and their lovemaking. It was an absolute dream when they were in bed together. She seemed to know instinctively what pleased him. They were so much in sync with each other, he couldn't believe his luck. How anyone would want to divorce her was beyond him. She was an angel in disguise.

***

The angel allowed the bath water to ease the tiredness from her limbs. She wouldn't be surprised to see bruises on her legs and body tomorrow. They'd made love franticly and feverishly without her having to reach top gear. Oliver was easy to please. He was a quantity over quality man. She could handle him at her leisure.

He was fun to be with, she had to admit. He got a bit intense now and then when at work, but take him to a pub or restaurant and stick a couple of glasses of wine down his neck and he became quite witty. He was certainly better material than her two previous husbands, and a darn sight better off, even accounting for the probable liabilities of his divorce. He was in line for promotion, too.

She felt that Oliver was enjoying himself with her, and

because he was the type of guy who seemed to put all his eggs in one basket, she felt that it was only a matter of time before he would want her to be with him on a permanent basis. That was fine with her. She could do wonders with the amount of money she'd have access to then.

She idly wondered about giving up working and spending winters in the West Indies. She would be able to meet lots of new people and make new friends who had influence.

She pulled the plug out of the bath but lay there until the water had drained away, and, along with it, any problems she might've had.

***

Katrina and Will had been showered and were getting ready for the evening meal. Katrina was relaxing a bit. She'd sent several texts to her father trying to assess Ella's mood. Despite knowing that Ella was trying to manipulate the weekend, it really affected Katrina that she was behaving like this. Katrina was reassured by the texts in return, which said that Ella was watching television and behaving normally – whatever that was these days.

Will had poured her some wine and it was good to relax in his company. This was their first official weekend and she was going to enjoy it – unless Ella kicked off again. Whatever happened was subject to the whims of her daughter in some way. After all, she was her responsibility.

Will dressed casually. His clothes were a good fit despite his fuller figure. He liked to think of himself as a good judge of a bottle of wine and a connoisseur of good food. This was his favourite type of evening – wine, food and excellent company. If the evening was rounded off by making love to the woman of his dreams, then that made it perfect.

They'd booked an early dinner for seven o'clock and he watched Katrina becoming more and more relaxed. Less than two hours later, they left the dining room and strolled hand-in-hand through the hotel grounds to an entrance door at the rear. They made their way to their room and quietly made love before falling asleep in each other's arms.

***

Oliver and Fiona marched into the dining room at nine having consumed a few drinks in the bar. They skipped the first course and went straight for the main course. They ordered a bottle of plonk and were soon finding everything in the room was just absolutely funny, including the other diners.

All *maître d*s have ways and means of getting rid of unwanted guests and this one was no exception. Within minutes of them completing their dinner, apologies were offered and technical difficulties in the kitchen were cited as reasons for disturbing them, and would it be possible for them to take their coffee in the bar?

It was, of course, no problem for Oliver and Fiona. The bar was their favourite haunt.

It was after midnight when they eventually went back to their room and peeled off their clothes. Oliver tried a quick fumble, but the vital organs weren't interested so they quickly got into bed and Oliver was snoring sonorously within seconds.

***

Will woke up during the night and gazed at Katrina lying on the bed. The moonlight was pooling around her face like a corona. She looked peaceful when sleeping; the lines only returned when consciousness kicked in.

He got up and looked out the window. An early morning mist lay shrouding the ground as though it was the stage of a theatre with dry ice eddying around for effect. Beyond the wall he could see the corner of the car park. A fox loped away from the hotel bins with something in its mouth. It disappeared into the mist like a mirage.

He poured himself a glass of water and sipped it, quenching the dry throat caused by last night's wine. He was at peace with himself and the world. He decided he was a lucky man.

***

Katrina woke to find Will in the shower and the sun streaming through the window. It was just after seven. She got up and peaked outside, using the curtains to shield her nakedness. The gardener was weeding a patch of newly turned earth. He's probably been there since dawn, Katrina thought

She decided to have an early breakfast and take a walk in the hills surrounding the hotel. A local information brochure showed several routes that were all gentle as far as terrain was concerned.

Will came out of the shower towelling himself, grinning. Katrina suspected he had carnal thoughts on his mind so she held up her hand as he walked towards her. "You can stop what you're thinking right now," she said with a look on her face that said she meant it. "We're going straight down for breakfast, then we're out for a long walk."

"Ok," he said. "Fine by me. We'll call into a village pub for lunch somewhere then make our way back. I'd like to spend some time in the steam room this afternoon if that's ok."

They stoked themselves up on a hearty breakfast, donned some robust boots and set out.

***

Fiona rolled over and extended her arm to touch Oliver. He wasn't there. She heard retching in the bathroom and the unmistakeable sound of someone evacuating their stomach contents through their mouth. She groaned. She didn't feel too grand herself but she wasn't as bad as Oliver appeared to be. Typical of a man, she thought, they always take things to excess. It didn't matter who they were, they ate too much, drank too much, tried to have sex and eventually heaved their guts up into a toilet bowl.

She waited a few minutes and decided to pretend she was concerned. She opened the door and was almost overwhelmed by the stench of vomit. Oliver was kneeling in front of the toilet with a string of saliva connecting his mouth to the bowl. His hair was matted with sweat. He was naked.

"Hello, love," Oliver said sheepishly. "That meal must've been a bit off last night. Got a bit of a dicky tummy this morning."

"Oh my poor darling," Fiona fawned. "Let's get ready and go downstairs. A big fried breakfast will put you right. Then you can take something for your tummy."

Oliver looked painfully at her while he considered her advice. His stomach started to convulse and he began throwing up again.

Fiona closed the door, rolled her eyes and went back to bed.

Shortly afterwards, Oliver staggered to the bed and joined her. They both went back to sleep and missed breakfast.

***

It had been a good walk. They were tired but feeling refreshingly healthy. They'd talked long and hard and sorted a lot of things, now it was time to relax and ease the muscles.

Katrina showered and elected to have a massage and facial.

Will headed for the steam room in the pool area and decided on a dip. The water felt good. He swam powerfully and stretched out as much as the pool allowed him. In no time at all he'd done fifty lengths. He climbed out and showered before padding down the corridor to the steam room. There was only one other person there – a blonde woman who briefly opened her eyes as he entered.

***

Oliver and Fiona had dragged themselves out of bed shortly before noon and eaten what Oliver called brunch.

Oliver had recovered well and was feeling a bit more sprightly, although he'd already decided that he wouldn't be drinking too much that night. He'd also decided to take a walk down to the local village and browse through the shops. He wanted to be back for the sport on television later.

Fiona had lazed around reading magazines and when Oliver came back, she'd told him she was going to "detox in the steam room".

She'd only been there ten minutes when the door opened and a tall, mature man entered. He was a bit flabby around the middle but he looked intelligent and handsome in a rustic sort of way, with a big friendly smile. He sat in the corner with a sigh and closed his eyes.

The room itself was a nine foot cube. It could take a dozen people, as long as they were sat up straight. There wasn't much room for legs. There were two tiers of benches on three walls.

A large thermometer was attached to the wall near the door, which had a six inch square window in it.

Will sighed. The warmth was lovely and he started to sweat profusely. He opened his eyes and saw the blonde woman looking at him. She smiled broadly. She was a good looking woman, in an obvious way. She wore a light blue bikini that was at least one size too small. Her breasts pushed out against the cups, which lifted them away from her body. They offered no support and were there for decency purposes only. He smiled back and shut his eyes again.

Fiona decided to have some fun. She groaned a little to make sure the man opened his eyes. She stood up and stretched, standing on her tiptoes, fingers pointed towards the ceiling. The bikini top couldn't contain her breasts under that amount of pressure and the costume slid up and off her. Her nipples bounded into view. She acted surprised but took her time to re-cover them. She selected a position directly opposite the man and lay back with her legs apart, still in an apparent gesture of stretching. She arched her back and lifted her knees and remained like that for a few moments before exhaling and softly moaning again.

Will couldn't believe what he'd just witnessed. Was this just a confidant woman stretching or was she some sort of exhibitionist? Could she be making a pass at him? He wasn't sure what to do. One thing was certain, he couldn't remain here; he felt deeply uncomfortable. But how was he going to make his exit? He could get up and walk out or he could ask her to be a bit more constrained – but that might be taken the wrong way. If he'd been interested and made a move, then that might be misconstrued as well.

He sat a few minutes rationalising his next move, hoping she wasn't going to do anything else. His agony was alleviated when the door opened and another man came in, someone about twenty years his junior. The blonde looked up at the young man and smiled. Will nodded politely at the newcomer and seized the opportunity to leave while the door was still open. He walked quickly away and changed back into his street clothes. He needed to tell Katrina what had happened.

Fiona smiled inwardly. The mature man had gone, replaced by this thirty-something man who was a better physical specimen. Let's try the same tactic with him, she thought.

***

Fiona returned to her room glowing. She poured herself a double vodka and coke and lay on the bed in her dressing gown. The detox had worked beyond her wildest dreams, now for the re-tox, as she called it.

Oliver was still watching sport somewhere.

***

Katrina listened to Will's story with amusement. The brazen hussy had been toying with Will, no more than that. It was the kind of thing women did when they were bored or had nothing going on in their lives. She'd teased Will remorselessly until they were ready for dinner at seven. They were hungry. The exercise and a pre-dinner gin and tonic had added edge to their appetite.

They devoured the paté and toast, the sea bass and vegetables, and were about to start on the crème brulèe when Will's phone rang. He excused himself and left the room.

Katrina pierced the crispy top of the crème brulèe and delved into its creamy interior. Will came back with a serious look on his face.

"That was Maria," he explained. "Her mother's died."

Katrina was stunned. She didn't know the woman, but she knew that her death removed the last obstacle to her marriage to Will. "How? When?" she spluttered.

"Maria went to take her to church this afternoon and found her dead in bed. They think it happened last night."

Will was plainly upset. He'd loved his mother-in-law during the early days. She had been a no-nonsense woman with a fiery Italian temper but capable of great gifts of generosity. She'd been the financial backbone during his formative marriage years, but her feelings for him had been tempered when she discovered Will and Maria's marital arrangement. It didn't fit in with her beliefs. However, her love for her sceptical grandchildren knew no bounds.

Will tried to renew interest in the meal but his heart wasn't in it. Katrina reached out and grabbed his hand.

"We're going home, Will. Maria needs you more than I do at the moment."

Will started to object but Katrina pressed on.

"We've got a lot of things off our minds today. I feel a lot better now we're heading in the same direction. You've got to go to Maria. I know how I felt when my mother died."

A tear appeared at the corner of Will's left eye. He couldn't speak.

"C'mon," Katrina said and stood up. They held hands as they left the dining room and went upstairs to pack.

***

Fiona had booked a table in the restaurant for nine o'clock. Oliver had been late back – something to do with extra time and a couple of pints of beer. More like four, she thought. So much for his declaration that he'd lay off the booze. She was ready, so she told him to meet her in the restaurant at nine.

She'd have a drink in the bar first.

Oliver reluctantly agreed, his thoughts of a quick shag before dinner thwarted.

Fiona hadn't been in the bar long before she was joined by a man in his thirties. Their chat was convivial and superficial. She looked at her watch and excused herself. She walked through the reception area and into the restaurant.

Oliver was late.

***

"That's her," said Will as he stood at the far side of the reception desk.

"Who?" said Katrina, her back to the restaurant.

"The woman in the steam room this afternoon." He pointed her out with a little nod of his head.

Katrina turned to look in the direction of Will's nod.

"Oh my God!" she said putting her hand to her mouth.

"What is it?" Will asked.

"It's Fiona," Katrina said. "Oliver's girlfriend."

"What?"

"It's Fiona, you know, the woman I told you about. The one that Oliver's seeing."

"It can't be," Will said. "Who's she with?"

Suddenly the lift doors opened and Oliver came scampering out and headed for the restaurant. He didn't notice Katrina, who was no more than twenty feet away.

Katrina fumed. Her husband had taken his floozy to the same hotel she'd been staying in with her lover. She said to Will, "Come on, let's go."

Her dream weekend had turned into a nightmare.

***

Harry lounged in his armchair trying to bring his foggy thoughts back to a level where he could focus on the day ahead. It had been a late night. Katrina had arrived at his house a little after midnight and had brought him up to date with the death and Oliver's assignation with Fiona. Well into the small hours, he'd offered her the spare room to stay what was left of the night. She'd accepted.

He mulled over the situation. The death of Will's mother had hastened the decision-making process. No longer was it a case that his daughter and Will couldn't get married because of Will's domestic circumstances, presuming that his wife kept her word and agreed to a divorce. Will would have to observe a brief period of dignified support for Maria until it became more appropriate for proceedings to take place. Katrina's usual dithering would be put under pressure.

He got up and looked out of the window. A fine rain was falling. It was the type of rain that had nuisance value rather than the sort that drenched or stopped outside pursuits. He debated whether or not to go to the park to feed the ducks, then decided he would as he'd be away for a week and this was his last opportunity. He got ready and went out clutching a bag of stale bread.

***

Katrina heard the back door close so she got up and looked out of the window. It was gloomy. She saw her father exit the gate with a bag in his hand. She smiled. He was on his way to the park. Some things in the world never changed. One of those things was her father's visit to the park. It was as if he thought the ducks wouldn't survive without him. She lay back down on the bed.

The previous twenty-four hours had moved her world further along the track more than she thought possible. Will's mother-in-law dying was a distressing incident that actually worked in her favour. She felt better now that Will could divorce Maria and be free to marry her. But that was still some way away.

The actions of Fiona in the steam room of the hotel demonstrated that she wasn't the woman for Oliver. Yet Katrina couldn't, or wouldn't, tell him in case it inhibited her own happiness. Oliver would get angry and accuse her of trying to destabilise his life anyway. He'd accuse her of hypocrisy. Yet she felt as though she still needed to say something. Her feelings for him still included caring for his welfare. She would hate to see someone take advantage of him.

***

Ella had heard the commotion through the night and knew her mother had arrived. Initially she'd been anxious, thinking something had gone wrong, but she'd crept down the stairs and listened to some of the conversation between her mother and her grandad. The cold and the fear of being discovered drove her back to the warmth of her bed, but she'd heard enough to appreciate that her mother would be marrying Will sooner rather than later and that her father was being taken for a ride by a tart. She fell asleep trying to think of a plan to thwart Fiona.

***

Harry returned home for lunch thinking that this time tomorrow he'd be in Spain. Katrina had made a sandwich and was chatting to Ella. There was no sign of the acrimony that had blighted their farewells when Katrina had left for the weekend. Harry knew that the incident had been bluff and bluster on Ella's part – a childish attempt to focus attention on her and not her parents.

They ate as a family, talking about superficial non-events that made them laugh. It harked back to bygone days, and it warmed them. When lunch was over, all three felt satisfied. The moment was broken only when Harry excused himself and went to pack for his holiday.

20

Harry sat on the plane reading a newspaper as best he could in the cramped conditions. He didn't remember it being as congested as this the last time he'd flown. Beside him, next to the window, was Hazel. She was reading *Les Liaisons Dangereuses* by Choderlos de Laclos, which surprised him. He didn't think she was the intellectual type. Was this going to be a holiday of constant surprises, he wondered.

On his other side was a sullen woman with an unfortunate face and dangling earrings. Her leathery skin was testament to many holidays lying on a beach without protection. He feared he would meet many like her.

Among his fellow travellers were two separate groups of young women who were having hen parties. One group of about fifteen wore black t-shirts that announced in graphic innuendo what their mission was once they'd reached their resort. The other group, perhaps more restrained, had their nicknames emblazoned across their chests. Both groups were raucous and partly drunk. It was eight o'clock in the morning.

Despite the cacophony generated by the self-proclaimed 'whores on tour', the journey was almost benign. The cabin crew remained calm and smiling throughout, their years of experience carrying them through just another day at work.

Harry and Hazel took a taxi from the airport and arrived at the hotel within half an hour. The sun was blazing down and Harry was sweating. The registration was relatively smooth, and within minutes they were in their room looking from the balcony over the beach to the Mediterranean Sea.

Their room was on the seventh floor and occupied a corner suite. It gave them views from the man-made marina that housed retail outlets, apartments and yachts of all shapes and sizes to the north, and the hotel lined promontory to the south. The Paseo Maritimo, swarming with fish restaurants and bars, swept beneath their hotel, linking north and south together.

Hazel disappeared back into the room and quickly returned with glasses of wine. She handed one to Harry.

"Here's to a wonderful holiday, Harry."

They chinked glasses and toasted each other. Harry put his arm around Hazel's shoulder and pulled her close. "There's me, and there's you. What more do we need to enjoy ourselves?" he said. Then, uncharacteristically, he kissed her on the lips. Not the passionate kind, but with just enough feeling to make them feel alive.

They remained there for several minutes watching the planes coming in to land at the airport they'd just left and then allowing their gaze to drink in their surroundings before unpacking and preparing to change into more appropriate clothing.

There was a shyness in Harry that made him want to change into his shorts in the bathroom, but Hazel grabbed him by the arm and turned to face him.

"Take your clothes off, Harry," Hazel said softly but firmly.

"What?" Harry said, not quite sure of what he'd heard.

"I said take your clothes off. I'm taking mine off."

She started undressing.

Harry watched her, puzzled, wondering what was going on.

"If we both take our clothes off and stand before each other naked, we'll not feel embarrassed for the rest of the week," Hazel said.

It was an off-the-wall suggestion that made a lot of sense. At some stage this week they'd planned to lie next to each other naked in any case. For that moment to have any majesty at all, they would have to be comfortable with each other, naked. They didn't want that moment tarnished by their own inhibitions.

Soon, they stood exposed to each other, yet their eyes remained locked. No-one spoke. Hazel took two steps forward and hugged Harry, still not saying anything. It was a lovely moment for them both. It was beyond respect and caring but just short of a declaration of a type of love not experienced by either of them before.

She kissed him on the lips and broke free. "C'mon, me darlin'," she said in a heavily accented Irish brogue. "Me belly thinks me throat's been cut. Let's find a place to have lunch."

They dressed in holiday clothes and left the hotel. They found a café just over the road. It was a pokey little place with televisions on every wall. Chalkboards with the house menu written on them hung facing the road to tempt itinerant tourists to eat there. Everything came with chips. They had a toasted sandwich, with chips, and a cup of tea.

"This is the first time I've been here since the last time," said Hazel.

Harry looked at her in surprise. He didn't think this place was a likely haunt for her. "When was that, then?" he asked.

"The first time? Or the last time?"

Harry shrugged. "Either."

Hazel sat back in her chair and raised her eyebrows. She

tilted her head to one side as if calculating the time span. "The last time was the first time," she said eventually, then added, "When I came here the first time, I said that it would be the last time. I didn't think there would be a next time." She vehemently nodded her head to accentuate the decision, "But here I am again."

Harry shook his head in amazement and said, "Hazel, sometimes I have no idea what you're talking about."

After lunch they took a brief stroll to familiarise themselves with their surroundings. They wandered down to a roundabout that had a host of multi-coloured windmills spinning in the warm, gentle breeze. They turned right, up the hill, to Paloma Park, where all sorts of fowl and birds wandered around. An enterprising local sold stale baguettes for one euro. Harry bought one and made his way to the lake. They spent ten minutes feeding the ducks, swans and everything that came close.

"*Paloma* is Spanish for dove," said Harry.

"That's interesting, although I can't see any," Hazel said looking around. "I can see everything else but a bloody dove. Look, Harry," she pointed at the water, "Terrapins."

A cockerel crowed from immediately behind her. Hazel gave a little scream in shock, to the amusement of one or two locals passing by. She grabbed hold of a laughing Harry. "C'mon, you bloody git. Let's go somewhere else."

They walked around the resort for an hour or so. She pointed out several places and features, declaring, "They weren't there last time I was here."

At three, they went back to the hotel, via the promenade. Harry sauntered on past the shops while Hazel popped into some that were selling souvenirs and cheap clothing. As they neared the hotel, Hazel caught up to Harry, looking a bit flustered.

"Harry," she said, "what's Spanish for frig off? Those people just won't give up trying to get you to eat in their restaurants."

Harry smiled. "I think if you say it in English they'll get what you mean. Some words don't need to be interpreted."

They went back to the hotel and had a siesta. They'd been up since five a.m.

The alarm went off after a couple of hours and they both took turns to shower and get ready for dinner. Harry wore a yellow checked short-sleeved shirt and tan trousers. Hazel wore a plain, pale-green dress. They both looked and felt good as they went to dinner.

The restaurant was reached by descending about two dozen steps from the left-hand side of the reception area. It held over two hundred people, and most of them were already dining. The head waiter welcomed them and took them to a table. He briefly explained the system and took their orders for drinks: *agua con gas* for Hazel and *agua sin gas* for Harry.

They ate three courses each. None of them were marvellous but all of them were satisfying. They left an hour later and made their way to the lounge, where the cabaret for the night was advertised as a tribute singer. They shrugged their shoulders and sat down.

The lounge was as big as the restaurant and was populated with round tables surrounded by four mock leather chairs. There was a dance floor and low level stage adjacent to the bar. Around forty people sat listening to piped music as a prelude to the main event. They were all older than Harry. A huge woman entered the room and sat down next to a man half her size.

Hazel nudged Harry. "Do you see her?" she said.

Harry looked.

"Did you see the amount of food she put away?"

Harry shook his head.

"I watched her. She brought seven platefuls of food to the

table with different things on them. She had a spare plate and she took bits and pieces from each of the others' to eat."

"Surely not?" said Harry.

"I tell you, she did. At one time she had so much food in her gob I thought she was breathing through her arse."

Harry laughed.

"Look at her. You couldn't bend wire that shape."

Harry laughed again, this time with a certain amount of embarrassment. He didn't like humour based on someone's appearance. He said so.

"That's fair enough, Harry. I'm not mocking her appearance. I'm remarking on her habits. She was eating as though a food shortage was going to be announced."

Despite himself Harry laughed again. He managed to catch the eye of the waiter, who sauntered across as though he was doing them a favour. He ordered a brandy for himself and a piña colada for Hazel.

Several more drinks followed, and when Elvis finished singing at eleven, they joined the exodus from the lounge and made their way back to their room. It had been a long day. They abandoned their clothes and crept into bed. They were so intoxicated that neither of them cared about hiding, or exposing, their bodies. They were tired and fell asleep instantly.

***

The moment Hazel longed for didn't happen on their first morning together as both of them had minor hangovers. They washed and dressed and just managed to make the restaurant in time for breakfast. Harry was ravenous, and thirsty. He ate a huge amount of bacon and eggs, with four slices of toast, and washed it all down with six cups of tea. Hazel selected porridge, fruit and toast, with a jug of coffee.

"She's here," said Hazel nodding towards the fat Spanish woman.

The woman lumbered in and Harry watched as she visited all the food counters. She selected meats, cheeses, croissants and half a baguette, and loaded them onto a variety of plates that she took to a table set for one. She then went back to the counter and selected some cakes and buns. Harry was amazed. If she ate all of it, it would be the most food he'd ever seen one person eat.

"My mother had a saying, Harry," said Hazel. "She used to say 'you know you're passed your very best when your belly's bigger than your chest.' In that woman's case, I think she's right."

Harry found himself gawping at the woman. She was eating like a crab; two hands stuffing food into her mouth in rotation.

It was too much for Hazel. "C'mon, Harry, let's go. I'm beginning to feel a bit nauseous."

They went back to the room and stood on the balcony.

"What shall we do today?" asked Hazel.

"Well, we could take a walk. You can show me around. Or we could sunbathe by the pool," Harry replied.

Hazel thought for a moment. "Let's do both. We'll sunbathe before lunch then walk this afternoon."

That set the tone for the next four days. The mornings were spent sunbathing and recuperating from the excesses of the previous night. The afternoons were reserved for walking, followed by a brief siesta. They became friendly with other couples and groups of people, all of whom were older than Harry.

***

On day five, Harry sat at breakfast with Hazel. She'd given various people nicknames, simply because she didn't know their real names. A woman with ginger hair became known to them as Ginger, and her husband was Ginger Tom. Later they found out he was called Bill. A good dancer was called Fred, and a woman with airs and graces became Mrs No Knickers, from the phrase 'fur coat and no knickers'. Another man was called The Toucher, after his habit of greeting people and touching the top of their arms. Another woman got the sobriquet Mrs Marbles from the way she talked. It was she who had just left Harry and Hazel at their breakfast table.

"What's with the eyebrows on that woman?" enquired Harry.

"What do you mean?" Hazel asked.

"When she was speaking to me her eyebrows were up and down like a pair of lifts. And she kept nudging me."

"She must fancy you."

"I don't think so. What makes you think that?"

"She thinks you're a bit of a goer,"

Harry's brow knitted "Whatever gave her that impression?"

"I told her last night that we make love at least twice a day."

Harry almost choked "What the hell for?"

"Just to shock her."

Harry shook his head. "The games people play," he said dismissively.

A flash of anger sparked in Hazel's eyes. "Yes, Harry, it is a game. When you're on holiday you can be who the hell you like. It's an escape from real life. At home you don't lie on the beach and get pissed every night. You don't fill your face full of crap. But when you're on holiday you do things you don't normally do. Pretending you're happy, or wealthy, or, in my case, being shagged to death, is part of the escape from what is usually a shitty life." She threw her napkin on the table and walked out of the restaurant.

Harry sat there, stunned. This was the first time he'd seen any temper in Hazel. He thought about what she'd said. He didn't usually subscribe to this lifestyle but here he was. Did everyone live a different life while on holiday? He didn't know.

The Incredible Bulk, the nickname Hazel had given to the fat Spanish woman, registered the incident with her eyes, but it didn't interrupt the rhythm of her arm movements.

Harry stayed downstairs for a few minutes and then went across the road to buy a newspaper. It gave him time to think. Hazel was right. He wasn't there to make judgements on anyone, and certainly not Hazel. Of course people were different on holiday. That was part of the fun.

He caught a reflection of himself in a mirror in the hotel's reception area. He was wearing a straw hat, a Hawaiian shirt, multicoloured shorts that reached below the knee, and a pair of leather sandals. Would he dress like this at home? No way! Even if it was a gloriously hot summer's day. He was dressed in the holiday uniform of a British subject abroad.

Hazel was lying on the bed when Harry returned to the room. He sat next to her, lowering his head in an act of contrition. "I'm sorry, Hazel," he said with genuine remorse. "I've upset you and made a fool of myself." She didn't respond so Harry continued. "Perhaps this is all too much for me."

She turned to him and smiled. "You're not used to letting yourself go, Harry, are you? You're so intent on doing the right thing that you've forgotten how to enjoy yourself. Do yourself a favour and lighten up." She raised herself up from the bed and put her arms around him. "You're a good man, Harry Crimson. I like you a lot. I love having you around. I know we get on well together. We wouldn't be here if we didn't. But we're bound to have differences that annoy each other. Doesn't everyone? We've just got to acknowledge them and move on." She paused briefly, then added in hushed tones. "Obviously, if people can't overcome their differences then they stop seeing each other."

Harry took hold of her and squeezed her to him. "I'm not letting you out of my life, Hazel … unless you want to go. I've found the kind of woman who makes me want to get out of bed every day, the kind of woman I miss when she's not there, the kind of woman who enriches my life just by being alive. I'm very fond of you, Hazel. You're right, I have to adjust. I've been so long by myself I don't know how to act like a couple again. I give advice to anyone and everyone and yet don't seem to be able to advise myself. Every now and then it takes someone dear to you to bring you back to the real world. That's what you are for me, Hazel, my window on the real world."

He sought her lips and kissed her passionately. Hazel responded.

Harry broke away from her. "Whoa!" he said. "I'm so sorry. Got a bit carried away."

Hazel grinned at him and said, "You've just demonstrated what I mean."

"How's that?" he asked.

"You didn't allow yourself the liberty of being carried away with your feelings."

"I made a promise to you, Hazel, and I'm well aware that we're coming to the end of a holiday and I haven't done what I said I was going to do. We've been so hung over and tired that we've never even felt like holding each other first thing in the morning."

"Ok," Hazel said, "I take your point. How about we do without the booze and have an early night tonight. It'll give

Mrs Marbles something to think about when we don't show."

Harry smiled his agreement.

Although the baking sun was high in the sky, the time for sunbathing was gone. They decided to walk the few kilometres along the beachfront walkway to Torremolinos, via the marina at Benalmadena. It was a lazy, leisurely amble to the resort, until they had to walk up the steep cobbled street to the bustling retail area. An hour or so window shopping led to a late afternoon lunch and a bus ride back to the hotel.

They still showered and dressed as if they were going down for dinner but they sat on the balcony looking over a still, inky blue sea. The moon was reflected on its surface. The air was warm and scented. Somewhere in the distance a variety of music was being churned out to entertain customers at a host of restaurants and bars. In the lounge, several floors below, the muffled melodies of the hotel's piped music wafted towards them.

"It's been a nice day," Hazel said softly.

"It has," Harry replied. They were holding hands. "About this morning …"

Hazel put her hand over Harry's mouth to stop him talking. "It's forgotten." She looked down at the garish collection of brilliantly lit eateries and said, "This time last week …"

It was Harry's turn to silence Hazel. "Remember," he said, "there's you, there's me and the here and now. That other world is somewhere else. And to be honest, at this moment I don't give a toss what's happening in it. It doesn't belong to us."

Hazel leaned across and kissed him. "You're right," she said. "Let's go to bed."

***

Harry lay there with Hazel. He listened to her breathing softly next to him. Her breaths were ruffling the hairs on his chest. They were both naked. They'd gone to bed and left the balcony door open. The curtains fluttered in the tiniest of breezes. It was a warm night.

For the past hour Harry had lain and watched the moon transit the heavens. He wasn't tired. He was bathing in the majesty of lying next to a woman who, at this moment, meant more to him than anything else. He'd thought guiltily of Thelma and times gone by. He felt a strange sense of wrongdoing, but surely it was right that he felt the way he did. A foggy confusion infiltrated his mind and sought to swamp his emotions. He briefly bordered on tears as anxieties ebbed and flowed like the sea outside.

He felt Hazel shift position. Her left hand came over his chest and she snuggled into him. He craned his neck and kissed the top of her head. She moaned appreciatively. He wrapped his right arm around her until his hand rested in the small of her back. She stirred. Her breathing came under control and she opened her eyes. She inched her way up the bed until their faces were level. Tears formed in their eyes as they hugged each other. Intuitively, they knew that this was the moment that Hazel had spoken about. The world outside the window no longer existed. They were in another place, the here and now, a timeless paradise reserved for those who care for another, a place where you and me were the only words that mattered.

21

The journey back home from the airport was a sombre occasion. They sat in the back of the taxi, hands clasped, allowing the real world to permeate their tans and make its way into their subconscious. The taxi driver's complaints of poor business and appalling weather quickened the transition.

Hazel elected to be dropped off first and told Harry that she didn't want him to come into the house. He knew that she, like himself, was having difficulty going her separate way. They exchanged friendly kisses while the taxi driver drummed impatiently on his driving wheel. Hazel disappeared inside as the taxi drove away towards Harry's house.

No-one was at home when he got there; he didn't expect there to be. The house seemed cold and uninviting. That was the first time he'd ever felt that way. Home had always been a haven for him, it was a place where he could curl up in warmth and comfort and feel safe in the knowledge that all was well. Something was missing, and he knew exactly what it was: its soul. He'd always believed that he was the soul of this house, but not now. He realised its soul was based on his love, and his love now lived on the other side of the park.

Suddenly he felt lonely and depressed. He unpacked, put his dirty clothes into the washing machine and then waited for the kettle to boil. He opened the curtains and windows to allow a brief circulation of fresh air before he could batten down the hatches to lock out the cool British summer.

He received a text from Hazel which said: *missing you already.*

The phone rang. It was Katrina. "Hi, Dad, just checking to make sure you got back safely."

"I'm back," he said, but didn't add what he was thinking: but I wish I wasn't.

"Did you have a good time?" she asked.

"I had a fine time," he said, "but I'm rather tired at the moment."

"Ok," she said. "Do you want me to keep Ella here until tomorrow? We can pop over for tea and hear all your stories then, if that's alright with you?"

"That's fine, Katrina," he said. "Is everything ok here?"

"I'll tell you what's going on tomorrow, Dad. See you then."

"'Bye, love," said Harry.

***

The next day dawned and Harry found himself lying in bed wide awake again. It had been forty-eight hours since he'd shared Hazel's dream moment, a moment that had had a profound effect on him also. He needed to speak to Hazel as soon as possible. There were things to be said.

He muddled along until ten o'clock – the time he went to feed the ducks. He was eager to get there, thinking perhaps Hazel would beat him to it. But as he neared their bench his heart sank. She wasn't there.

Just as he sat down, he received a text from Hazel saying that when she'd got home there'd been a letter from the hospital asking her to attend that morning for an appointment. It had arrived the day they'd set off for Spain. She hadn't had time to cancel or re-arrange it, so she was going today.

Harry cursed his luck. Today of all days. He opened up his bag and started tearing at the bread. He failed to spot Mistress Duck on the lake. He hoped she hadn't been taken by a fox or something. But her friends came, quacking, screeching and squawking; swimming this way and that; waddling along the lake's edge, jostling for position; swooping from the sky to steal any bread not yet devoured by the swans.

He watched the feeding frenzy to the end. Then calm returned. He looked around the park. Hardly anyone was there. Maybe everyone was at work, or school, on holiday, or they had something else to do. At that moment he felt like the loneliest man in the world. He liked his own company, but he realised that it was much nicer to have someone in your life. Someone you could talk to, even if it was just to say, "looks like rain again".

He sighed and left the bench to walk home, a short journey that seemed to take forever.

***

At teatime, Katrina and Ella arrived. Ella skipped through the front door and hugged Harry tightly. "Glad to have you back, Grandad," she said in delight. "Wow, look at your tan. You look so healthy!"

Harry smiled and kissed them both. "I had a great time." He laid his hands on his paunch and said, "I've put on a few pounds. I've never eaten and drank so much in my life."

Ella said, "And how is Hazel?"

"She's fine," Harry replied. "She's been terrific company."

Katrina sat down on the sofa. "How was the hotel?"

"Much like any other hotel," Harry said, "nothing spectacular, but it did have a great view."

Katrina coughed politely. "And … umm … did Hazel get what she wanted?"

Harry shook his head at the obvious inference but took a diplomatic tact. "We had a great time," he said. "Absolutely fabulous. So what happened here?"

Katrina noticed the change in conversation and let it pass. "Fine," she said. "A lot's happened since you went away."

"Ok, let's have some tea and you can tell me all about it."

Tea lasted two hours. Katrina gave Harry a brief précis of the series of events that had happened in the past week, followed by some more in-depth information.

Will's mother-in-law's service had taken place yesterday. A full Catholic Mass had been followed by burial at St Boniface's. Katrina had declined an invitation to attend as Will's partner, to allow him and Maria to present themselves as man and wife for the last time. Maria had agreed to a divorce as soon as it was decent to do so. Katrina's solicitor had filed a motion for divorce and initial contact had been made with Oliver's solicitor. Neither solicitor expected substantial disagreements and predicted an early settlement.

Ella became bored with the conversation at this point and went upstairs to her room.

Katrina said that she'd seen Oliver through the week. He'd mentioned that he was looking at Fiona as a long-term relationship and, when Katrina had pressed, hadn't dismissed marriage as an option.

Katrina hadn't mentioned the steam room incident to Oliver, deciding that Oliver had to find out what Fiona was like all by himself. That would be the only way he would accept it. Besides, her concern for his welfare came second to her need to ensure that the divorce went smoothly and an amicable settlement was reached. Keeping Oliver sweet was central to that, and Fiona was actively keeping him sweet, at least for the time being.

The company that had been granted the contract for the revamp of the town centre had gone into administration, and the estimation for the process of tabling bids from other companies would take months. The demolition of the charity shop and its neighbours had been put back indefinitely. That meant Will, and Katrina had time to cement their relationship before any pressure was put on them through a forced move.

Katrina said that she and Ella had sat down for two nights in a row last week and discussed their situation. It had been a tearful and honest exchange of views and the subject of where Ella should stay had been decided. She was returning to live with her mother this weekend.

"Wow," said Harry, "It's been an eventful week for you." He could've added: and me.

"It has," Katrina replied.

"Are you happy, love?" Harry asked.

"Not quite, Dad, but I'm getting there. There's still a lot of shit to wade through before I can say I'm happy."

"So Ella's going home."

"Yes. She loves being here, Dad, but, without any pressure from me, she decided that she wanted stability and a taste of her old life rather than staying here. Is that ok with you?"

He'd miss her of course, but he nodded. "It's the right place for her to be," he said, "at home with her mother. What about Will?"

"We've decided that now the pressure's off we can control our own destiny to a certain extent. He and Maria are going to sell their house and Will is keeping the money from its sale. That's his settlement. There's also a few thousand in the bank.

Maria's mother has left her house and estate to her. She's an only child." She leaned back into the sofa. "As far as Ella is concerned, we've decided that we'll not share a house until she's comfortable with it."

Harry raised his eyebrows. That put Ella in control, and that was a flaw in the plan.

Katrina noticed her father's expression and addressed it. "I think Ella is growing up. We reckon that when she sees Will and me together, which will be almost every day, she'll become accustomed to him. We're sure she'll start to like him. I've told her I see my future with him. She might not like it, but she'll have to get along with it."

Harry noticed the steely determination in her voice. Only time would tell if the plan worked.

"You seem to have covered everything," said Harry.

"We'll see," Katrina said, "but at least everything is out in the open now. No more secrets." She paused, went over to Harry and hugged him. "I'm sorry I lied to you, Dad. I was under so much pressure I didn't know what to do. Can you forgive me?"

He squeezed her tightly. "Someone said to me recently that shit happens. They were right. Lies breed more lies, and eventually someone gets hurt. If you love someone enough, then you'll do anything for them."

It was then that it hit him. A couple of days ago he'd hugged Hazel and admitted that he'd given advice to all and sundry, yet found it difficult to take his own advice. He'd just said to Katrina that if you loved someone enough, then you'd do anything for them. So why wasn't he with Hazel now? Why, when she'd gone to hospital, for whatever reason it was, and he didn't know, was he not with her? Why weren't *they* sitting down and talking about *their* future together?

"Dad?" said Katrina.

Harry was shaken out of his thoughts. "Sorry, love, I was miles away."

"With Hazel?" she enquired.

"Yes," he said. He let go of Katrina. Tears misted his eyes as he sat down again. "We kind of connected when we were away. I like her a lot."

Katrina knew from her own recent experience that it was an emotion a great deal more than 'like' that was troubling him. She swallowed hard. This was a difficult question to ask her father. "Did you and her ...?" She couldn't bring herself to ask it.

"Have sex?" Harry shook his head. "No. I made her a promise and kept it. But I'll tell you this, I wish I hadn't."

"You want to see more of her?" Katrina asked.

Harry nodded. "Yes, I do. I want to see a lot more of her."

"You should go to her now and talk things over. I presume she feels the same way?"

"I think so," Harry said.

For two straight talking people like Harry and Hazel not to have communicated their feelings was a nonsense, and Harry felt angry with himself.

The doorbell rang.

Harry went to answer it and saw a policewoman standing there.

"Mr Crimson?"

"Yes."

"Mr Harry Crimson?"

"Yes. That's me." A feeling of dread squeezed his heart. When does a policewoman knock on your door? It could only be bad news. His mind raced through a legion of scenarios in a split second but came up with nothing. "What's the matter?" he asked anxiously.

"Can I come in, sir?"

Harry stood to one side and allowed her into the hall. He ushered her into the lounge and waited.

Katrina stood up and said, "What's the matter?"

Ella scampered down the stairs and appeared around the corner. "Who's …" her question frozen by the sight of the policewoman. She sidled up to her mother.

"We've had a call from the hospital. Do you know a Mrs Hazel O'Shea?" she asked.

Harry almost choked. "Yes, I do," he said in a strangulated voice.

"I'm afraid I have some bad news, sir."

"Oh my God!" Harry winced. "What is it?"

"I'm sorry to inform you, sir, that Mrs O'Shea had an operation this afternoon to remove an aneurism from her abdomen. Regrettably, the aneurism burst. The doctors were unable to control the situation. Unfortunately, Mrs O'Shea died in the operating theatre."

Ella shrieked.

Harry's world exploded. He collapsed into his chair.

Katrina went to comfort him.

"Oh my good God," cried Harry. "Hazel, Hazel, Hazel, why didn't you tell me?"

"I'm sorry for your loss, sir. I only have the information I've given you. You'll no doubt want to know more. I have a telephone number for you to call." The policewoman handed over a piece of paper. "Is there anything else I can do for you?" she enquired.

Katrina took charge. "No thank you, officer. I'll take care of things from now on."

She showed the policewoman to the door and thanked her once again, then returned to find her weeping father comforting Ella who was sobbing violently. The picture frightened her. Only a few moments ago her father was on the point of confessing his love for a woman, and now she was gone. She went to the hall phone and rang the number on the piece of paper. She spoke briefly to a nurse and returned to her father.

"They want you to collect her things. Apparently she put you down as her next of kin should anything go wrong."

Harry wiped away his tears. The initial shock was gone. He dug deep into his famous stoic pragmatism. "Right," he said," I'm off to the hospital."

"I'll drive you," said Katrina.

He shook his head. "I need to do this myself. Anyway, you'll need to look after Ella. It's not a place for her to be." He lifted up Ella's chin and gazed at her tear filled eyes. "You see, Tuppence, it's important to make sure that those you love know it, because they won't be around forever." He picked up his car keys and walked towards the door.

"Dad," implored Katrina.

He waved away her protestation and left.

22

Harry's heart was heavy as he made his way to the hospital. He'd made this journey several times over the years and he found himself parking in the same spot as he'd done the last time he was here – a routine appointment for himself.

He quickly found the ward he was looking for and approached a nurse. He identified himself and was taken into a room where he was left briefly until he was joined by a doctor who introduced himself as Dr. Buchanan.

"Hazel had been undergoing some routine gynaecological tests recently," the doctor said, his spectacles balanced precariously on the end of his nose, while leafing through the file. He found the appropriate place. "Ah, yes," he said, "here it is. Her abdomen was scanned and an abdominal aortic aneurysm was found."

"A what?" said Harry. "Listen, Doctor, my brain isn't quite functioning as well as it might. You're going to have to explain it in words I can understand."

The doctor noted Harry's distress and confusion. He took a deep breath. "An aneurysm is a bulge in a blood vessel wall. Sometimes the blood vessel wall has a weakness. As blood passes through the weakened blood vessel, the pressure causes it to bulge outwards like a balloon."

Harry nodded his understanding.

The doctor continued. "Aneurysms can occur anywhere in the body, but one of the most common places is in the abdominal aorta, and that's where Hazel had hers."

"How does this sort of thing happen?" Harry asked.

The doctor explained. "There're lots of causes – smoking, high blood pressure, there's even a hereditary link. The simple answer in Hazel's case is we don't know. The abdominal aorta is the largest blood vessel in the body. In most cases, an abdominal aortic aneurysm causes no noticeable symptoms and does not pose a serious threat to health. However, there's a risk that a larger aneurysm could rupture. A ruptured abdominal aortic aneurysm can cause massive internal bleeding, which is usually fatal."

Harry cradled his head in his hands.

"Are you ok, Mr Crimson? Do you wish me to continue?"

"Yes," said Harry. "I'm sorry. All of this is a bit of a shock, that's all. I didn't even know she was ill."

The doctor continued. "When the aneurysm was discovered, her doctor told her that the size of it indicated that preventative surgery was necessary. The aim of that kind of treatment is to prevent the aneurysm from rupturing. This usually means replacing the weakened section of the blood vessel with a piece of synthetic tubing. However, preventative surgery carries a small risk of causing serious complications. It's usually only recommended if it's thought that the risk of a rupture is high enough to justify the risk of surgery. In Hazel's case it was.

"The size of the aneurysm is often used to measure the risk of rupture. Preventative surgery is often recommended for an aneurysm larger than 5.5cm. That was exactly the size of Hazel's aneurysm."

"Could it have ruptured at any time?" asked Harry.

The doctor nodded. "If she hadn't had the scan she wouldn't have known. It could've gone at any time."

"But she knew she had the aneurysm?" Harry asked.

"Yes, she did. That's why we invited her in fairly quickly." The doctor closed the file. "Is there anything else you want to know, Mr Crimson?"

Harry shook his head and said, "What happens next?"

"The hospital will have someone who will liaise with you. I'm sorry for your loss, Mr Crimson."

He stood up and Harry shook his hand before he left.

***

Harry drove home in a bit of a daze. On the back seat was a bag that held Hazel's clothes and her handbag. He had no idea what to do with them. Someone at the hospital was going to contact him during office hours the next day. As next-of-kin he had the authority to dispose of Hazel's remains, and that threw up a whole host of problems

It was dark when he arrived home. He parked his car in the drive and sat looking at his house. It looked forlorn and desolate. Tears welled in his eyes and dribbled down his cheek. Soon, huge, shoulder jerking sobs racked his body and he beat the steering wheel with both fists. His wails were confined to the car.

A neighbour walked his dogs past the bottom of his drive without noticing him. Life elsewhere carried on as normal.

It was almost an hour before Harry left the car.

He entered the house, put the hospital bag on the sofa and called Katrina to tell her what had happened at the hospital.

"I'm so sorry, Dad," she said, and cried.

"Is Ella ok?" Harry asked.

"She's here, Dad. I thought it best to bring her home. She's very upset."

It promised to be a lonely night.

It turned out to be a sleepless one.

***

The new day broke. It was serene and quiet. The dawn chorus had been replaced with a dignified silence. The sky was clear and the first rays of sunshine promised a lovely day.

Harry made breakfast. He didn't quite know what else to do. Should he contact the hospital? Should he wait until they contacted him? The sight of the hospital bag overwhelmed him with sorrow. He opened it. The smell of Hazels perfume wafted up from her dress, permeating the room as if she were standing there. He could almost hear her voice. "That's not the first time you've had that dress off me."

He held the material against his face and breathed the scent, comforted by it. He gently took the contents out of the bag. He opened her large, brown leather handbag. The usual woman's paraphernalia were stored in various zipped compartments and different sized pockets. There was a diary.

He opened the diary and found the entry for yesterday. It said: *Hospital to fix balloon.* Despite himself, he smiled. That was typical Hazel.

He read the previous week's entry: *Benalmadena – holiday.*

Further back still she had written: *Fino died. Funeral. Scan.*

She was a woman of few words when it came to diary-keeping, Harry thought absently.

Her purse contained cards, keys, coins and bank notes amounting to around £50. The last place he looked was the zipped central pocket. In it he found a sealed envelope. It was addressed to him.

The last thing he expected to find was something addressed to him. His fingers trembled. He sat down in his chair and stared at the envelope. It was plain and cream-coloured with his name written in blue ink half way down in Hazel's handwriting. He took a deep breath and opened it.

It was letter with yesterday's date at the top.

A sudden burst of emotion panicked him. He stood up. He couldn't bring himself to read it. He put it down and went outside into the garden to calm his anxiety. This was all a bit too much for him. This time yesterday he was supremely happy. He had intended to tell Hazel that she meant the world to him. Indeed, if she'd reciprocated in the way he thought she would, he'd confess that he thought he was in love with her. How could things go so badly wrong?

He took some deep breaths to calm his nerves. Once composed, he went back inside the house, picked up the letter and read it.

Dear Harry,
You probably think I'm daft for writing this letter but you know me – just in case. I'll probably keep it and show you one day.

Anyway, I'm going into hospital today for a minor operation to fix a balloon that's attached itself to an artery. It's straight forward but it carries a risk that it might burst. If it does I probably won't wake up. At least I won't know anything about it.

I had the cheek to tell the hospital that you were my next of kin. I hope you don't mind. I haven't got anyone else. That's not to say I wouldn't choose you if I had, if you know what I mean.

I had a great time on holiday. I loved being with you. You and I worked well together. For the first time in a lot of years I felt as though I was with a man who I could spend the rest of my life with. Although given the difference in ages, the rest of your life. Ha! Ha!

The past few years have been shit for me. If I hadn't met you feeding the ducks in the park that day I don't know what I'd have done. If it hadn't been for you I think I would've topped myself when Fino died. You gave me hope to carry on.

If the worst happens and I don't make it, I want you to take charge of things for me.

I love you Harry Crimson.
XXXXX

PS
My house keys are in my purse. In the wardrobe in my bedroom is a box file with everything you need to know in it.

The phone rang. It was the hospital.

A brief conversation revealed the intricacies of recovering Hazel's body. Essentially, an undertaker took care of it all, but the top and bottom of the situation was that Harry was in charge. He had the final say.

Exactly what Hazel had wanted.

23

Harry sat on the park bench feeding the ducks.

He cut a lonely figure throwing scraps of bread towards the water. All sorts of birds swarmed around him to receive their regular feed. He'd fed many generations of these birds over the years and in return they'd given him a great deal of pleasure. There was one duck in particular who was almost feeding from his hand. He called her Beatrix.

Today was a special occasion. It had been exactly five years since Hazel's death. Five years to that very moment when he'd expected to see her sitting on this bench feeding the ducks, the day after their holiday in Spain. Instead, she'd entered hospital to have an operation that would result in her death.

He'd tried to take control of Hazel's affairs, but that had been thwarted by officialdom. He'd gone to her house and endured the profound grief that came with looking through a deceased loved one's possessions. He'd had great difficulty sifting through things that meant everything to their owners but nothing to him. He'd seen a photograph, presumably of Fino, in her bedroom. The expression on his face seemed to say 'Who are you? What are you doing?'

He'd put it in a black sack to be thrown away.

He couldn't find any photos of Hazel by herself that had

been taken in the years since Fino had been institutionalised. Who would've taken them? Fino was all she'd had until Harry came along.

He'd found the box file and opened it. It held her Will. There was a letter starting 'To whom it may concern'. It instructed the finder to inform Mr Reginald Bresslaw of Barnaby, Bird and Bresslaw, Solicitors, in the event of her death. He'd done so immediately. He wished he hadn't.

Mr Bresslaw was the Executor of the Will, and, in his official capacity, ordered Harry to leave the house immediately and could he be so kind as to drop in the keys to the house at their chambers in High Street.

Harry had done as he was told. He arranged the funeral and was the only one who attended the crematorium. Mr Bresslaw had paid the bill.

Hazel's house was sold and he never found out what happened to her estate. He had nothing of hers to remind him of their times together, except some wonderful memories and an aching heart.

He emptied the bag of crumbs on the ground and put the bag into the rubbish bin. He walked quickly back home. He was expecting to have lunch with Katrina and Will. He was hoping Ella would be there now that she had graduated.

Katrina and Will had married the weekend before Ella started studying Law at Durham University. They'd sold their respective houses and pooled resources to buy a modern house on the edge of town. They'd also secured a shop premises in the newly built Town Centre Regeneration Project. They were delightfully happy, and it showed. Will was a really nice guy and he adored Katrina.

On one or two occasions in the past, in conversations with Harry, Katrina had mentioned her divorce. Harry reminded her that the reason she'd divorced in the first place was to reestablish herself as a person in her own right and not be classed as a wife, mother or daughter. She'd argued that it was her decision to accept those roles and that made it ok. He'd smiled. You can twist words any way you wish when the need arises.

Will's relationship with Ella had been precarious at first, but it had blossomed quickly. At one stage, Ella deliberately stayed with friends so that her mother and Will could spend time together. Then one day Ella called a family summit and announced it was ok by her if Will stayed the night. One night led to weekends, and the weekends got longer, until Will asked Ella if she had any objections to him moving in. She'd hugged him and given her blessing. The fact that she was away at University made it easier.

Ella matured rapidly at Durham and became a fine student. She spoke to Harry often and occasionally stayed with him on her sojourns home. She'd noticed that her grandad had become a little more introspective and always gave her advice about 'taking her chances when they came' and 'never putting off 'til tomorrow what you can do today.' Recently, she'd noticed he had an empty look behind his eyes, a look that had replaced his big, smiling, grandad eyes.

Oliver had married Fiona with a great deal of pomp and ceremony, and they'd honeymooned in St. Lucia. Their dream home was only partially built before Fiona had left him for the CEO of a textile firm. Nevertheless, resilience was one of Oliver's key qualities. He now lived in the next street to Katrina with a plain looking woman called Jayne, who worshipped him. Oliver and Katrina's relationship remained amicable.

By the time Harry reached home he was out of breath and exhausted. He quickly got ready and was coming downstairs when the doorbell rang. He opened it and Ella rushed in and flung her arms around his neck.

"Surprise!" she said excitedly.

He was pleased to see her. He looked behind her but couldn't see Katrina or Will. "Where's your mother?" he asked.

"They're at the restaurant. I've come to get you," she replied. "There wasn't enough room in the car for all of us."

"There's only four," Harry said.

"There's five. I've brought someone I'd like you to meet."

"Oh!" said Harry.

She walked back to the front door and signalled to someone in the car. Harry heard the clunk of the car door and footsteps making their way up the path. A young man with sandy coloured mop-hair appeared. He almost filled the doorframe.

"Grandad, this is Jake, Jacob really. We were at Uni together."

Harry proffered his hand. "Pleased to meet you Jake. Call me Harry."

"Jake graduated at the same time as me. His dad's a Queens Counsellor in London. We're both going to work for him," she said by way of explanation.

"Oh! So you're both colleagues, then," he said mischievously.

She blushed. "Grandad," she said. "We're going to be, but ..."

"He's your boyfriend," he finished.

Jake was grinning. "We got on from day one," he said. "We've been together for about a year or so."

Harry sized him up to be the gregarious type. Fresh-faced, raw-boned and healthy. He liked him immediately.

"C'mon then," said Harry as he ushered them out of the house. "Tell me all about yourself on the way to the restaurant."

They all ate a hearty lunch and shared a couple of bottles

of wine. Ella was the nominated driver and drank water. She dropped off Will, Jake and her mother at home and took Harry back to his house.

"He's a fine young man, Ella. It's a bit early for you to be settling down, though," he said,

"I know that, Grandad," she replied, "but he's the first man I've actually fallen in love with." There was a moments silence then Ella spoke again. "You once told me that I would meet someone special some day and he would float my boat," she smiled at the expression, "in ways I couldn't even imagine."

He smiled at the memory,

"You were right, Grandad. I now know what love is about. I now recognise love in other people. I see Mum and Will together and know they're in love. I see Dad and Jayne. I don't know about him, be she loves him to bits." She paused. "I can't remember much about Gran," she said furrowing her brow, "but I do know that you loved Hazel very much. It was you who couldn't see it," she said.

He was shocked. No-one had said that to him before, but she was right. He looked out of the window and said absently, "I did. I should've told her." He remembered the letter she'd left him. "I think she loved me, too."

"Do you remember that fairy story you made up about Inkarta, Estraneo and Lela?" she said.

He smiled again. "Yes, I do. It wasn't very good, was it?"

She laughed out loud. "I remember it was terrible," she said. "But it got me thinking. It took my mind off what was going on. I didn't realise you were trying to tell me things about my life, and life in general."

"Fairy tales help us make sense of the world," he said.

She nodded and sighed. "Ok, Grandad," she said picking up her bag and keys. "I'm off back to Mum's." She kissed him and said, "I love you."

"I love you, too, Tuppence," he said. "Keep your eyes open for dragons."

"And fairies!"

He waved goodbye as she drove away.

***

Three hours later, Harry was feeling uncomfortable with the food and drink he'd consumed, and although he felt tired, decided to take a walk through the park. He grabbed some biscuits and crunched them up to take for the ducks. He locked up and walked down the street. He turned right, then left. The park gates loomed in front of him once again. He was beginning to feel the effects of indigestion long before he reached his bench for the second time that day.

It was as if Beatrix had sensed his return. She was waiting on the edge of the lake. Harry sat down and opened his bag.

Beatrix waddled backwards and forwards as if worrying that Harry might grab hold of her. She came nearer and nearer his outstretched hand. Harry didn't move. Beatrix was within inches of his fingertips. A crumb fell off his hand and landed on the ground. Beatrix dashed forwards and snapped it up immediately. It seemed to give her confidence. She ventured nearer. There were many more crumbs in the palm of Harry's hand. With trepidation she went closer still, and closer, until she lowered her head to guzzle the crumbs from his immobile hand. Other ducks wandered over to inspect what was happening. A pigeon landed on Harry's shoulder. Harry remained immobile.

A couple walking their dog near the lake saw Harry on the bench and rushed over. One of them rang for an ambulance, but it was a waste of time. It was obviously too late.

The ducks swam away.

Epilogue

The young woman pushed her twins in their pram through the park towards the lake. A bag of stale bread lay hidden under the covers, with a brass plaque and four screws.

This was her tenth annual visit, her first with her children. She picked up the bread and started crumbling it into pieces for the ducks. Birds swooped in from all angles thrilling the wide-eyed children who giggled and clapped at the spectacle.

Some starlings and sparrows sat on the branches of a tree next to the bench, a tree the young woman had planted five years before without permission. It was almost a crime, as far as any self-respecting lawyer was concerned, and she was about to commit another.

She took the plaque and centred it on the back of the bench. She drove the four securing screws firmly into place and stood back to read it.

Harry and Hazel
forever feeding ducks

The young woman smiled through her tears. Her children looked at her in wonder. She pushed the pram towards the gates, turned and took a long last look at the plaque.

"'Bye, Hazel. 'Bye, Grandad," she said.

A dozen ducks silently stood to attention in front of her. Then, in the blink of an eye, the ducks parted and allowed her through. Ella strode out of the park and took the young Harry and Hazel home.

Lightning Source UK Ltd.
Milton Keynes UK
UKOW05f0124110214

226254UK00006B/59/P